HOPETOWN

By Beverly Johnston

Acknowledgements

Thank you to those who inspired my characters in this book—whether through your kindness, wisdom, or simply by being a part of my life. Your influence helped shape these characters and bring their journey to life. This story would not be the same without you."

Special Thanks to

My husband Eric Johnston

and

The lady who shared her story of the Mustard Seed

This book was written using AI with my storyline plot.

Some scenes are based on real events

Others are merely fiction

Prologue

The small town of Hopetown had always been a place where life moved at a gentle pace. Seasons rolled in and out with a familiar rhythm, and the people who called it home found comfort in its quiet streets and close-knit community. It was a place where stories unfolded not in grand, sweeping gestures, but in the quiet moments—the stolen glances, the whispered dreams, the slow healing of hearts that had been broken.

Julia never imagined that she would begin her life over here, far from the shadows of the past she had once believed unshakable. She hadn't planned for change. But change, as she would come to learn, had a way of finding you whether you were ready or not.

Her journey wasn't marked by a single moment, but by a series of them—the decision to leave, the kindness of strangers who became family, the quiet strength of a man who would teach her how to trust again. It was a story of resilience, of love found in unexpected places, and of learning to believe in oneself when the world had tried to convince you otherwise.

And yet, as much as love had been a gift in her life, so too had loss. Because love, at its deepest and truest, was never just about beginnings. It was about the willingness to cherish, to fight for, and ultimately, to let go when the time came.

This is Julia's story. A story of love, of heartbreak, and of the quiet, unshakable faith that carried her through it all.

HOPETOWN

By Beverly Johnston

**

Chapter 1

At just 24 years old, Julia felt far older than her years. She had married Ed straight out of high school, believing in the fairy tale of love and happily ever after. By 21, she was a mother to Sarah, her bright-eyed little girl who was the only true light in her life. But now, just a few years later, Julia found herself questioning everything. The love she once felt for Ed had eroded under the weight of his temper, his indifference, and the growing sense of isolation that filled their home. Was this really the life she was meant to live? Or had she made a mistake that she was only now beginning to see clearly?

Julia leaned against the kitchen counter, her fingers clutching the edge as if it could keep her from unraveling. The hum of the refrigerator was the only sound in the small, dimly lit space. A plate sat untouched on the table, its contents congealing under the faint yellow light of the overhead bulb. Sarah's giggles echoed faintly from the living room, a bittersweet melody that seemed to mock Julia's inner turmoil.

Ed had left again, slamming the door hard enough to rattle the windows. The echo of his last words lingered in the air like smoke. "You're useless, Julia. Can't even get dinner right," he had spat, his eyes cold and unrelenting. She had barely managed to hold back tears until he stormed out. Her arms still ached from the bruise he left the night before when she'd tried to stop him from yelling at Sarah for spilling her juice.

The worst part wasn't his words. It was the weight of their truth, or at least how much she believed them in the quiet moments after he was gone.

A couple nights before, in a rare attempt to rekindle something, anything, Julia had bought a new nightgown. She'd hoped the soft lavender fabric and lace laying against her youthful slender figure would remind Ed of the young couple they used to be. She had spent time curling her brunette hair that fell just below her shoulders, feeling confident that Ed would be pleased. When she walked into the bedroom, his reaction had been anything but pleased. "What are you trying to prove? You look like a tramp in that," he had sneered, shaking his head. "Don't embarrass yourself, take that shit off."

Julia had retreated to the bathroom, hot tears spilling down her cheeks as she clutched the nightgown to her chest. She'd stuffed it into the back of a drawer, vowing never to wear it again. That memory still burned fresh in her mind as she stared blankly at the untouched plate of food on the table.

"Mama?" Sarah's voice pulled her from the fog. Julia turned to see her now three year old daughter standing in the doorway, clutching a stuffed rabbit with one ear hanging by a thread. Her bright blue eyes and light blonde hair were a stark contrast to the shadows that loomed over their lives.

"Yes, sweetheart?" Julia managed, forcing a smile that didn't quite reach her eyes.

"Can I have some water?" Sarah asked, her voice soft and cautious. Julia nodded and filled a glass from the faucet, handing it to her daughter with trembling hands.

"Here you go," she said, brushing a strand of Sarah's hair behind her ear. "How's Mr. Hoppy doing?"

"He's okay," Sarah replied, looking at her rabbit. "But I think he needs fixing."

Julia knelt down to Sarah's level, placing a gentle hand on her daughter's cheek. "I'll fix him for you tonight, okay?"

Sarah smiled, a small beacon of light in the gloom. "Thanks, Mama."

As Sarah padded back to the living room, Julia sank into one of the kitchen chairs. She pressed her palms against her face, trying to push away the exhaustion that clung to her like a second skin. Her mind wandered to the unopened sketchpad buried in the closet. It had been years since she'd touched it, but lately, she found herself thinking about it more and more—especially during the darkest moments.

She glanced at the clock. It was nearly midnight. Another day survived, though it felt like she was merely enduring, not living. Julia's gaze drifted to the window, where the faint glow of the moon peeked through the curtains. Somewhere out there, she thought, there had to be a different life—a better one. But for now, it was just a dream, as fragile and frayed as the threads of Mr. Hoppy's ear.

**

The morning sunlight streamed through the blinds, painting the kitchen walls in thin strips of gold. Julia stood at the sink, rinsing a few dishes, her mind replaying the events of the night before. The house was still quiet, except for the soft ticking of the wall clock and the occasional rustle of movement from Sarah's room. It was a rare moment of peace, and Julia clung to it like a lifeline.

She glanced at the stack of mail on the counter. Among the bills and advertisements was a flyer for a local community center. The bright colors and bold letters announced a series of art classes starting next week. Julia's eyes lingered on it, her fingers itching to pick it up. But she hesitated, the weight of doubt pressing down on her.

"Good morning, Mama." Sarah's voice broke the silence. Julia turned to see her daughter rubbing sleep from her eyes, her stuffed rabbit tucked under one arm.

"Morning, sweetheart," Julia said, wiping her hands on a dish towel. "Did you sleep well?"

Sarah nodded, sliding into one of the kitchen chairs. "What's for breakfast?"

"How about some pancakes?" Julia offered, her voice lighter than she felt.

Sarah's face lit up. "Yes, please!"

As Julia busied herself mixing batter, she stole glances at the flyer. The thought of picking up a paintbrush sent a strange mix of excitement and fear coursing through her. Could she really do it? Could she carve out a piece of herself in a life that seemed to revolve around survival?

After breakfast, Julia folded the flyer and tucked it into her purse. It was a small act, almost impulsive, but it felt like a spark—a tiny flicker of hope that she couldn't quite extinguish.

By mid morning, Julia was at work in the diner, the scent of frying bacon and freshly brewed coffee mingling in the air. She tied her apron tighter around her waist and grabbed her notepad, ready to take another table's order. The familiar clatter of dishes and low hum of conversation provided a backdrop that, while far from glamorous, felt stable in its own way.

It was here that she first met Charles. Charles Schiff was a man who carried both wisdom and warmth in equal measure. At 34, he was a full decade older than Julia, yet there was a youthful energy about him, an effortless charm that made him seem timeless. He was clean-cut, always well put together without appearing overly polished. His neatly trimmed beard framed a strong jawline, and his deep-set, thoughtful eyes held the kind of intelligence that came from both book smarts and life experience. He was sitting alone at the counter, a newspaper spread out in front of him and a cup of coffee in hand. His smile was warm, and his easy confidence immediately set him apart from the other customers.

"Hi there," he said as Julia approached, his voice gentle but steady. "What's the special today?"

She returned his smile, albeit cautiously. "Meatloaf and mashed potatoes," she replied, pen poised over her notepad. "Or we've got a great BLT."

"I'll take the BLT," Charles decided, folding the newspaper. "And maybe a refill on this coffee?"

"Coming right up," Julia said, turning to grab the coffee pot. As she poured, she noticed his eyes lingering on the small doodle she had absentmindedly sketched in the corner of her notepad.

"Is that yours?" he asked, nodding toward the sketch.

Julia blinked, surprised. "Oh, uh, yeah. Just something I do to pass the time."

"You've got talent," he said, his tone genuine. "Ever thought about doing more with it?"

Julia felt her cheeks flush. "Not really. Life's… busy."

"Well, you should," Charles said, his eyes meeting hers. "The world could use a little more beauty."

Something about his words stayed with Julia long after she walked away to place his order. For the first time in months, she found herself smiling without forcing it.

**

That weekend, Julia visited her mother, Sarah skipping happily beside her as they walked up the worn stone path to the modest brick home where she'd grown up. The air was thick with the scent of roses, her mother's pride and joy, blooming in the front garden.

"Grandma!" Sarah exclaimed as the door swung open.

"Sweetheart!" Julia's mother, a petite woman with neatly styled graying hair, bent down to embrace her granddaughter. Her smile faltered only slightly when her gaze shifted to Julia, whose weary expression was hard to miss.

"Hi, Mom," Julia said, forcing a smile.

"Come in, come in," her mother said, ushering them into the cozy living room. Sarah immediately darted off to the small corner where her toys were kept, leaving Julia and her mother alone.

Over tea, Julia's mother studied her closely, her brows furrowing. "You look tired, Julia. Is everything alright?"

Julia hesitated, her fingers tightening around the warm cup. “I’ve been… stressed. Things with Ed have been hard lately.”

Her mother sighed, setting her cup down with a gentle clink. “Marriage isn’t easy, Julia. It takes work. Your father and I had our struggles too, but we stuck it out.”

Julia looked down at her hands, the faint bruise on her wrist hidden by the long sleeves of her blouse. “This feels different, Mom. Sometimes, I don’t know if I can keep going.”

Her mother reached across the table, her hand warm and steady on Julia’s. “You have a daughter to think about. Children need both their parents. Ed might be rough around the edges, but he’s a good man at heart. You just need to find a way to reach him.”

Julia bit the inside of her cheek to keep from snapping back. A good man? The words echoed in her mind, mingling with memories of Ed’s cutting remarks and heavy-handed outbursts. But her mother’s well-meaning advice only deepened the guilt that already weighed on her.

“I’ll try,” Julia said finally, her voice barely above a whisper.

Her mother smiled, seemingly satisfied. “That’s all you can do, Julia. Marriage is about compromise and perseverance.”

As they prepared to leave, her mother handed her a container of homemade cookies. “For Sarah,” she said with a wink. “And remember, you can always talk to me if you need to.”

“Thanks, Mom,” Julia murmured, hugging her goodbye. But as she walked back to the car with Sarah’s hand in hers, her mother’s words sat heavy in her chest. The idea of “reaching” Ed felt impossible, like trying to catch smoke with her bare hands.

**

That evening, Julia sat alone at the kitchen table, the flyer spread out in front of her. Sarah was already asleep, her soft snores drifting down the hall. Julia traced the edges of the paper with her fingertips, her heart tugging between the desire to take the class and the fear of stepping outside her comfort zone. It seemed foolish, indulgent even, to think about art when her life was so fractured.

The sound of the front door slamming made her flinch. Ed's heavy footsteps followed, and soon he appeared in the doorway, his face flushed and his jaw clenched.

"What the hell is this?" he barked, snatching the flyer off the table. He held it up, waving it like a piece of evidence. "Art classes? Are you serious? Since when do you have time for crap like this?"

Julia's stomach twisted. "It's just a flyer," she said quietly, avoiding his gaze. "I haven't signed up for anything."

"Good," Ed snarled, crumpling the paper in his fist. "Because we don't have money to waste on your stupid little hobbies. You think painting's gonna fix this mess of a life? Grow up, Julia."

Her hands clenched into fists in her lap, nails digging into her palms. She wanted to argue, to tell him how much it meant to her, but the words stuck in her throat. Experience had taught her that fighting back only made things worse.

Ed sneered at her silence. "That's what I thought," he said, tossing the crumpled flyer onto the floor. "Clean up this mess," he added before stomping down the hall to their bedroom.

Julia stared at the crumpled paper for a long time, her chest tight with anger and shame. When she finally moved, it was to smooth the flyer, a small act of defiance that only she would know about.

**

Ed's anger had always been a constant in their marriage, but it wasn't until years into their relationship that Julia began to understand where it came from. She had caught glimpses of his past in the way his shoulders tensed at certain noises or how he sometimes clenched his fists without realizing it. He didn't talk much about his childhood, but the few stories he'd shared painted a grim picture—a picture Julia could never quite forget.

Ed grew up in a small, run-down house on the outskirts of town. His father, a foreman for a construction company, had been a man of towering strength and even greater temper. "A man's man," people in their neighborhood had called him, though Ed's memories of the man were far from admirable. His father had been quick to anger and quicker to act on it. Ed still remembered the sting of the broom handle and the booming voice that seemed to shake the very walls of their home.

As a boy, Ed learned early on to stay out of his father's way. He'd tiptoe around the house, holding his breath whenever his father came home after a bad day. The sound of the front door slamming shut was like a warning siren—a signal to retreat to his room and stay silent. But sometimes, no amount of silence could save him.

"You call that a clean floor, boy?" his father had roared one evening, his heavy boots thudding against the creaking floorboards. Ed, no older than ten, had stood frozen in the kitchen, a broom clutched tightly in his hands. He had scrubbed the floor for hours, his small hands sore from the effort, but it hadn't been enough.

Before Ed could explain, his father had yanked the broom from his hands and swung the handle down across his back. The sharp crack of wood meeting flesh echoed through the room, and Ed collapsed to the floor, gasping in pain. "Maybe next time, you'll learn to do it right," his father had spat before walking away, leaving Ed crumpled on the cold linoleum floor.

His mother had tried to shield him when she could, but there was only so much she could do. Ed's father was a storm, and no one could stand in his way for long. When his father's wrath turned on her, Ed would clench his fists until his knuckles turned white, powerless to stop it.

The worst part wasn't the bruises or the shouting—it was the quiet moments afterward, when his father would sit in his chair as if nothing had happened. "A man's gotta be tough," he'd say, his voice steady and firm. "The world doesn't respect weakness."

Those words had lodged themselves deep in Ed's mind, shaping the man he would become. He'd vowed as a teenager to never be like his father, but the lessons of his childhood were hard to unlearn. He carried them with him into adulthood—into his marriage. The anger that had been displayed by his dad had made a boy poisoned as a man, spilling over into his interactions with Julia and Sarah.

Ed's job in construction didn't help matters. The long hours, the physical demands, and the constant pressure to meet deadlines left him perpetually on edge. His crew's mistakes became his responsibility, and the weight of that responsibility often felt unbearable. Every missed measurement, every delayed shipment, every call from an irate client seemed to add another layer to his simmering frustration. He brought that frustration home with him, unable to leave it at the job site.

Julia saw the toll it took on him, though she doubted he'd ever admit it. She saw it in the deep lines etched across his forehead, in the way his hands trembled when he thought no one was looking. She tried to reach him, to offer comfort, but her attempts were often met with resistance.

"I don't need your pity," he'd snap, pulling away from her touch. "Just… let me be."

It wasn't that Ed didn't love Julia or Sarah. In his own way, he did. But love, for Ed, was tangled up with control and fear. He didn't know how to express it without reverting to the patterns he'd grown up with. And so, the cycle continued—anger, regret, and a fleeting promise to do better, only for the cycle to start again.

One night, after a particularly bad fight, Ed sat alone in the darkened living room, his hands resting on the coffee table. Julia and Sarah were asleep, or at least pretending to be. The house was silent, but his mind was anything but. He thought about his father, about the life he'd sworn to leave behind. He thought about Julia's tear-streaked face, about the fear he'd seen in Sarah's eyes.

What am I doing? he wondered, his chest tightening with a mix of anger and shame. He didn't want to be his father, but he didn't know how to be anyone else. The realization hit him like a punch to the gut, leaving him breathless and hollow.

For a fleeting moment, he considered reaching out—to Julia, to a counselor, to someone who could help him break the cycle. But the thought was quickly drowned out by a familiar voice in his head: "A man's gotta be tough. The world doesn't respect weakness."

And so, he stayed silent, his hands clenched into fists as the shadows of his past closed in around him.

**

Julia lay in her bed, her hands trembling slightly as she traced the hem of her worn nightgown. The silence of the house felt oppressive, broken only by the occasional creak of the old wooden floorboards. The moonlight filtering through the thin curtains cast faint shadows on the walls, their shapes shifting like restless ghosts. She stared down at her gown, where her fingers absentmindedly twisted the fabric, her thoughts a chaotic whirlwind she couldn't silence.

She had tried—God, how she had tried. For years, she had poured every ounce of herself into their marriage, into making Ed happy, into keeping the peace. She had listened to her mother's advice, over and over like a broken record: "Marriage isn't easy, Julia. You have to work at it. Men have their ways, and it's a wife's job to understand them."

But what if those ways broke her? What if the weight of understanding crushed the very core of who she was?

She glanced toward the dresser, where she had recently placed her sketchpad hidden beneath a pile of folded laundry. It seemed like forever since she'd opened it, since she'd allowed herself even the smallest indulgence of drawing. Every time she thought about it, guilt clawed at her. How could she sit and sketch when there were dishes to wash, floors to scrub, and a husband to placate? But lately, the urge to create had grown stronger, a persistent whisper in the back of her mind.

Tonight had been another fight. Not a physical one this time, but the words had cut just as deeply. She had mentioned the art class again, her voice tentative, as if testing the waters.

"I was thinking," she had said during dinner, "maybe I could sign up for that watercolor class at the community center. It's only one evening a week, and—"

Ed had slammed his fork down, the sound making both her and Sarah jump. "A waste of money," he had barked. "We've got bills to pay, Julia. Or did you forget about those?"

"I didn't forget," she had whispered, her appetite vanishing. "I just thought… it might be good for me. To have something that's mine."

He had laughed then, a cold, sharp sound that made her chest ache. "Yours? Everything in this house is yours, Julia. The roof over your head, the food on the table. What more do you need?"

What more do I need? The question had echoed in her mind all evening, a bitter reminder of how small her world had become.

Now, alone in the dark, she let herself feel the weight of it all. The loneliness. The frustration. The faint glimmer of hope that refused to be extinguished, no matter how many times she tried to snuff it out. Her hand drifted toward the bedside table, where a small photo of Sarah smiled back at her. Her daughter's bright eyes and infectious grin were a reminder of why she stayed, why she endured. Sarah deserved a stable home, a family. Julia had promised herself she would give her that, even if it meant sacrificing her own happiness.

But tonight, something inside her had shifted. It wasn't a dramatic moment, not a thunderclap or a revelation. It was quiet, like the first crack in a dam.

That night, Ed came to her in a way that felt different at first. His hands, usually rough and demanding, moved with an unexpected gentleness. For a fleeting moment, Julia let herself believe—hope—that maybe things were changing. Maybe this was the man she had fallen in love with years ago, the man who used to hold her with care.

She responded cautiously, desperate for something that resembled love, something that would make her feel like a wife again instead of just a fixture in Ed's life. But as soon as she let her guard down, the tenderness faded.

"You want something of your own?" he muttered, his voice dripping with venom. "Here ya go, bitch."

Before she could react, the shift was complete. His grip tightened, his movements turning harsh and punishing. The weight of him crushed her against the mattress as each thrust sent pain tearing through her. She gasped, trying to shift away, but his hands clamped down on her wrists, trapping her beneath him.

Tears burned in her eyes, but she refused to let them fall. She had learned long ago that showing weakness only made it worse. So she bit her lip, staring at the ceiling, willing herself to disappear into the cracks of the paint, into the silence that had become her refuge.

It was over as suddenly as it had begun. Ed rolled off of her, sighing like he had just finished some exhausting task, then turned his back to her as if she were nothing more than an afterthought.

Julia lay there, frozen, her body aching, her heart hollow. A single, undeniable thought echoed through her mind—she had to leave.

She didn't know when or how, but she knew this: she could not live like this anymore.

Trying to think of anything other than what had just happened, wet drips rolling from her eyes, she thought about the sketchpad again, about the feeling of a pencil in her hand, the way the world seemed to fade away when she lost herself in a drawing, wishing she could feel that way in this very moment. It had been years, but the memory of that peacefulness still remained.

Her thoughts turned to Charles, the man who always seemed to notice her in ways no one else did. His comment about her talent had stuck with her, replaying in her mind like a song she couldn't forget. Maybe he was wrong. Maybe her drawings weren't worth anything. But the way he had said it, with such certainty, made her wonder if there was something she had overlooked about herself.

She closed her eyes, and a memory from high school surfaced—a day she had been so proud of a piece she'd drawn in art class. It was a portrait of her mother, shaded meticulously with pencil. When she'd shown it to her mom, she'd been met with a polite smile and a dismissive comment: "It's nice, dear. But don't you think you should focus on something more practical? Drawing won't pay the bills."

The sting of those words had lingered for days, and over time, moments like that had piled up. A teacher once told her she had potential, but when Julia shared her dream of becoming an artist, her friends had laughed. "Good luck with that," one had said. "You'll be broke before you know it." Those memories now swirled in her mind, mixing with her current doubts. She was terrified of trying again, of failing in a way that would prove all those voices right. What if her art really wasn't good enough? What if Charles only encouraged her out of pity?

Julia listened to see if Ed was sleeping yet. His heavy breaths confirmed that he was. Slowly, she rose from the bed and padded to the dresser. Her hands hesitated for a moment before pulling out the sketchpad. It felt heavier than she remembered, as if it carried the weight of all the years she had ignored it. She moved cautiously with every step to the living room..

A faint creak in the hallway snapped her out of her thoughts. She froze, her heart racing, but the sound passed, and the house returned to its oppressive silence. She flipped it open, the soft light of the night light left on for Sarah was just enough light to see the drawings, her breath catching at the sight of her old drawings. They were rough, amateurish, but there was a spark in them, a glimmer of something she had forgotten she possessed—a sense of identity, a quiet hope, and the freedom to be something beyond what her life had confined her to. She traced a finger over one of the sketches—a tree with branches that twisted like veins—and felt a lump rise in her throat.

Maybe it was foolish. Maybe Ed was right. But as she sat down on the sofa and picked up a pencil, for the first time in years, Julia allowed herself to hope.

**

The next day at the diner, Julia moved from table to table, her smile polite but distant. The clinking of dishes and the hum of conversation buzzed around her, but her mind was elsewhere. She had slipped the sketchpad into her bag that morning, almost as an afterthought, but now she couldn't stop thinking about it. It sat in her locker in the back, waiting, and the thought both thrilled and terrified her.

After the lunch rush subsided, Julia found herself sitting at the counter during her break, staring absently out the window. A crumpled receipt and a pen lay in front of her, but she hadn't touched them. The diner's fluorescent lights buzzed faintly, the hum merging with the muffled conversations of lingering customers. Her hands rested on her lap, but her fingers twitched slightly, betraying the nervous energy coursing through her.

Her thoughts spun with the same questions that had haunted her the night before. How could she leave? Money was the first hurdle, an insurmountable wall that loomed over her every time she dared to think about escape. The diner job barely paid enough to cover groceries, let alone rent or childcare. She had no savings to speak of, and the idea of asking her mother for financial help made her stomach churn. Her mother's lectures about sacrifice and staying the course would only make her feel more trapped.

Julia's gaze shifted to the sketchpad in her bag, hidden but not forgotten. Could her art somehow be the answer? The thought felt absurd, almost laughable, but it clung to her like a stubborn ember refusing to die. She thought of Charles's words, his quiet encouragement. "If it makes you happy, you should do it." Was it naive to believe that something as simple as a pencil and paper could open a door she hadn't even dared to knock on?

She sighed and leaned her elbows on the counter, burying her face in her hands. For the first time in a long time, the weight of her situation felt almost unbearable. But even in the depths of her doubt, a tiny voice inside her whispered, urging her to try—to find a way, any way, to carve out a life that felt like her own.

Later that night, as Julia lay in bed staring at the ceiling, the weight of her thoughts pressed down on her chest. The room was dimly lit by the glow of the streetlamp outside, its pale light casting faint patterns on the walls. Beside her, Ed's steady breathing signaled that he was asleep, oblivious to the storm raging inside her.

The idea of leaving had crossed her mind more times than she could count. Tonight, after her mother's stern lecture about staying in her marriage and Charles's gentle encouragement to embrace her art, the thought loomed larger than ever. But the question that always followed, cold and sharp, was how?

How could she walk away from the life she had built, imperfect as it was? How could she uproot Sarah, leaving behind the only home her daughter had ever known? And then there was the practical side—money, housing, support. She had a job at the diner, but it barely covered groceries and small expenses. Without Ed's income, how would she afford rent or childcare?

She closed her eyes, but the flood of abusive memories wouldn't stop. She saw herself fumbling with numbers, struggling to balance the checkbook while Ed dismissed her concerns as if they were her problem. She remembered the nights she stayed up late, staring at bills she couldn't pay, wondering how she had ended up in this life. The weight of responsibility pressed heavily on her chest, leaving her breathless. She wanted out, but the logistics of leaving seemed impossible, like scaling a mountain with no gear and no map.

Her mind wandered to the quiet research she had done during her break at the diner. There were shelters for women leaving abusive relationships, some offering temporary housing and counseling. She had scribbled the number for a local hotline onto a napkin, tucking it away in her pocket like a secret lifeline. Government assistance was another possibility—food stamps, childcare vouchers, maybe even help finding an affordable apartment. But the process seemed daunting, a bureaucratic maze she wasn't sure she had the strength to navigate.

And then there was Sarah. How would she explain it to her daughter? How could she promise a better life when she wasn't even sure she could provide one? Julia felt her eyes well up, the tears spilling over and tracing warm lines down her cheeks. She bit her lip to stifle a sob, not wanting to wake Ed. Even if he knew she was leaving he wouldn't understand, wouldn't care. He would only see her tears as another weakness to criticize.

She thought again of Charles's words, his belief in her talent, his gentle insistence that her happiness mattered. The contrast between him and Ed was stark, like night and day. With Charles, she felt seen, valued. With Ed, she felt invisible, her worth reduced to how well she kept the house and soothed his anger.

Julia wiped her tears with the edge of her sleeve and turned her head to look at the sketchpad on the nightstand. It had become a symbol of possibility, a spark of *hope* she couldn't entirely extinguish, no matter how much doubt clouded her mind. If she could just summon the courage to leave, to start over, maybe that spark could grow into something real—something lasting.

But courage was in short supply tonight. As the clock ticked on and the room grew darker, Julia curled into herself, clutching the edge of the blanket as if it could shield her from the uncertainty of tomorrow. She told herself that she would figure it out, that she would find a way. For Sarah, for herself. Because the alternative—staying—felt like slow suffocation, a life half-lived.

Somewhere in the house, the radiator groaned, and Julia took a deep breath, letting the sound anchor her. The journey ahead seemed impossible, but for the first time in a long time, she felt a flicker of determination. Tomorrow was another day, another chance to search for a way out, another chance to reclaim the pieces of herself she had lost.

**

Each day passed with Julia's anxiety about Ed's behavior growing more unbearable. On this particular night, Ed came in late, full of rage, though she had no idea why. She tried to keep her distance and stay silent, choosing instead to spend the evening snuggling with Sarah in her room. Together, they read books about princesses and puppies, the moments almost dreamlike in its warmth and comfort. It felt like a fleeting glimpse of the life she wished for, one filled with love and peace. But the serenity shattered as soon as Sarah fell asleep and Julia tucked her in with a gentle kiss on her cheek.

Julia softly walked to the bedroom to change into her nightgown, hoping the quiet would grant her some peace. Ed stormed in, his face twisted with anger. He accused her of ignoring him all night, his words venomous and loud. "You're an awful wife, Julia. Absolutely useless," he spat, his voice growing more menacing with every syllable. She tried to speak, her voice trembling as she apologized, but before she could finish, his hand shot out, striking her across the face with a full fist.

The impact sent her reeling, tiny white lights flickering in her vision as pain radiated through her skull. Staggering, she instinctively turned to leave the room, but Ed shoved her hard against the wall, pinning her with his weight. Tears streamed uncontrollably down her cheeks as she slid to the floor, her back scraping against the wallpaper. Curling into herself, she wrapped her arms tightly around her knees, as if creating a protective shell that could shield her from his rage.

Ed's verbal assault continued, each word cutting deeper than the last. "You're nothing without me," he sneered, looming over her. Then, to her horror, he unzipped his pants, his contempt reaching a sickening crescendo. He stood over her as his warm, acrid stream hit her head, running down her face and soaking into her clothes. Julia sobbed uncontrollably, her body trembling as humiliation and fear enveloped her. When he finished, Ed zipped up and walked away without a glance back, muttering, "Pathetic. You're less than nothing."

Julia remained on the floor, drenched and broken, unable to move. The walls of the room seemed to close in, suffocating her with the weight of what had just happened. As the sound of Ed's footsteps faded, a single thought pierced through the haze of her despair: This has to end. She couldn't live like this anymore.

Julia sat on the cold bedroom floor, her arms wrapped tightly around herself as she rocked slightly, trying to steady the tremors wracking her body. Her nightgown was still damp, clinging to her skin like a second layer of shame. The scent of urine lingered, mixing with the salt of her tears, and she choked back a sob. Her breath came in shallow gasps, her chest rising and falling in erratic bursts as she fought the overwhelming tide of emotion threatening to drown her.

She had endured so much before—verbal attacks, manipulation, even bruises hidden beneath layers of clothing—but this? This was something else. This was dehumanizing. This was Ed breaking her in a way she wasn't sure she could piece back together.

Her fingers dug into her arms as a flood of thoughts crashed over her. I have to get out. I have to go. I can't stay here. I won't survive this.

But even as the resolve formed, a new fear took its place. How? Where would she go? How would she take Sarah and make sure they had a roof over their heads? Would he even let her leave?

She needed a plan. Something real. Something that wasn't just a desperate thought in the middle of the night but an actual way out.

With slow, deliberate movements, she pulled herself up, her knees shaking beneath her. She made her way to the bathroom where she reached for a washcloth, scrubbing at her skin until it burned, as if she could erase what had just happened. When her hands stopped shaking, she pressed her forehead against the cool mirror above the sink, forcing herself to breathe. Wiping off just wasn't enough, she stepped into the shower and stood under the warmth of the water hoping that all of Ed's anger he had excreted over her would somehow wash away. She had spent the last week secretly researching resources—hotlines, shelters, legal aid—but she hadn't yet taken any real steps forward. She had told herself it wasn't the right time. That she needed to be sure. But now? Now, she had no more excuses.

A shelter could provide temporary housing, but the thought of bringing Sarah into a space filled with strangers, living out of a shared room, made Julia's stomach knot. Still better than here, a small voice reminded her. And she knew it was right.

She thought of the number she had tucked inside her purse, written in rushed, shaky handwriting on the back of a diner receipt. A women's crisis hotline. She had stared at it for days, but tonight, it felt like it might be her only lifeline.

Her mind raced through everything she needed to do. She had to gather documents—Sarah's birth certificate, social security cards, anything important. She needed to stash money, whatever little she could skim from grocery runs and tips at the diner. She needed to figure out when Ed would be gone long enough for her to leave without him stopping her.

And then there was Sarah.

Julia bit her lip hard enough to taste blood. How would she explain it? How could she prepare her daughter for something so drastic without scaring her?

She closed her eyes and pictured Sarah's bright, curious face, her innocent questions about why Daddy was so mean. Julia had lied to her, sugar coated things, made excuses. But no more. I won't let her grow up thinking this is normal. I won't let her think this is love.

Her jaw clenched with newfound determination.

Tomorrow, she will make the call.

Tomorrow, she will take the first real step toward freedom.

The next morning, Julia moved through the diner like a ghost, her body going through the motions while her mind raced with plans. Every time the cash register opened, she made note of the crumpled bills customers left behind, wondering how much she could set aside without raising suspicion.

She couldn't take money straight from the till—if she was caught, she'd lose her job, and then she'd have nothing. But her tips… those were hers. She started pocketing the smallest bills throughout the day instead of adding them to the communal tip jar, careful not to take too much at once. She would need cash—money that Ed couldn't track through their bank statements.

Between orders, she discreetly jotted down a list on the back of an old receipt:

- **Documents** – Birth certificates, social security cards, IDs
- **Cash** – As much as she could quietly stash
- **A place to go** – Shelter? A friend? Cheap motel?
- **Transportation** – Bus schedules, routes out of town

The weight of the list pressed down on her, making the act of writing feel heavier than it should. She had never done anything like this before—never planned an escape.

At the end of her shift, she asked Margie, the older waitress who had worked at the diner for years, if she knew of any cheap places to rent.

Margie gave her a long look before responding. "Why? Are you thinking of getting a place on your own?"

Julia forced a small, tired smile. "Just… looking at options."

Margie didn't pry, but there was something in her eyes that said she understood more than Julia had intended. "Well, places around here ain't cheap, but sometimes there's rooms for rent. Might be better than a full apartment right off the bat. You need help, you let me know."

It wouldn't be much, but it would be something.

**

Later that night, when Ed was dozing off in front of the television, Julia quietly retrieved a small box from the back of the closet. Inside, she stuffed a few of Sarah's clothes, some of her own, and a small envelope where she had started tucking away her extra tips. It wasn't enough yet, but it was a start.

Tomorrow, she will check the bus schedules.

Tomorrow, she will call the hotline.

She wasn't ready yet. But soon… soon she would be.

**

The following afternoon, Julia stood behind the counter at the diner, absently wiping down the same spot on the counter as her thoughts raced. Her body ached, her wrist still sore from Ed's latest outburst. She had covered the faint bruises with the cuff of her uniform, but she still felt exposed, as if everyone could see right through her.

"Hey," Charles's voice pulled her from her thoughts.

She looked up quickly, her pulse jumping before she forced a small smile. "Hey."

Charles leaned against the counter, his eyes scanning her face. He always seemed to study her in a way that made her feel both seen and vulnerable. Today, his expression darkened. "You okay?"

Julia's fingers clenched around the rag in her hands. Lying came so easily now. "Yeah, just tired."

Charles didn't look convinced. He glanced down at her wrist, where the faint outline of a bruise was just barely visible beneath the cuff of her uniform. His jaw tightened. "You sure about that?"

Julia swallowed hard, dropping her gaze. She wanted to confide in him, to tell someone—anyone—the truth. But saying it out loud would make it real, and she wasn't ready for that yet.

Before she could answer, the bell above the diner door jingled, and Julia instinctively straightened, ready to take the next order. Charles hesitated but didn't push her any further. Instead, he pulled out his wallet and slid a twenty across the counter.

"For coffee," he said. "And keep the change."

Julia frowned. "Charles, that's too much—"

"Just take it." His voice was gentle but firm. "Consider it an investment in your art."

Her breath hitched. Art. He was always reminding her of that part of herself, the part she had tried so hard to bury. She stared at the bill for a moment before slowly tucking it into the pocket of her apron, her fingers trembling slightly.

She didn't thank him out loud. She couldn't. But she hoped he could see it in her eyes.

**

Julia's Escape Begins

That night, after Sarah had fallen asleep and Ed had passed out in his recliner, Julia sat at the kitchen table, her wrist still throbbing. She cradled a cup of decaf coffee between her hands, staring at the dark liquid as if it held the answers she so desperately needed. She had spent the day thinking, running through every possible scenario, every risk, every consequence.

Her car.

She had been so focused on shelters, on aid programs, on legal steps, that she hadn't let herself consider the simplest answer—she already had a way out. Her car wasn't much, an old sedan that rattled when it hit forty-five, but it was hers. The title was in her name, a small miracle considering Ed liked everything under his control. If she could just get in and drive—far enough that he wouldn't come looking—she could figure out the rest later.

She grabbed a notebook and flipped to a blank page, pressing the pen to the paper with a shaky hand.

Step 1: Where to go.

Her cousin, Rick.

She hadn't spoken to Rick in years, not since before Sarah was born, but he had always been the kind-hearted type. Growing up, he had been like an older brother to her, always watching out for her when no one else did. Last she heard, he managed a small mobile home park a state away. He had mentioned once that vacancies came and went, and she prayed one was open.

With shaky hands, she picked up her phone and searched for his number. When she found it, her stomach twisted. Would he even pick up? Would he remember the way he used to promise to look out for her?

Taking a deep breath, she tapped the call button.

After a few rings, a gruff but familiar voice answered, "Julia? Damn, it's been a while."

Her throat tightened. "Rick… I need help."

There was a pause, then his voice softened. "Tell me what's going on."

"I—I can't stay here anymore. With Ed. It's bad, Rick." Her voice cracked as she tried to speak quietly so as to not stir Ed from his sleep, and she swallowed the lump in her throat. "I need to get out, but I don't have anywhere to go."

He exhaled sharply. “Say no more. I’ve got a trailer open, nothing fancy, but it’s got a roof, heat, and a lock on the door. If you can get here, it’s yours.”

Tears welled in her eyes. “Really?”

“You think I’d turn my back on you?” His voice was firm, no hesitation. “You get yourself here, Jules. I’ll make sure you and Sarah have a safe place to land.”

Relief flooded through her so suddenly she nearly dropped the phone. “Thank you, Rick. I—I don’t even know what to say.”

“Just get here in one piece,” he said. “And don’t tell that bastard where you’re going.”

Her grip on the phone tightened. “I won’t.”

Step 2: Money.

She had no savings, but she had tips. Tonight, before leaving the diner, she had pocketed most of what she earned instead of leaving it in the house jar like she normally did. It wasn’t much, but it could cover gas and a couple of cheap meals. A few more weeks like this and she’d have a decent stash, at least enough to get to Rick’s.

She thought of Charles’s twenty-dollar bill, still tucked into her apron pocket. He had called it an investment in her art, but now it was an investment in her escape.

**

Confiding in Charles

The morning rush at the diner had slowed to a lull, the hum of conversation now just a soft murmur between customers. Julia wiped down the counter absently, her mind racing with everything she had to do before she left.

She had already stashed away her tips from the morning shift. She had spoken to Rick, confirmed the trailer was ready. The plan was in motion, but she had to be careful—every detail had to be right before she made her move.

She needed to tell someone.

And she knew exactly who.

**

Charles sat in his usual spot at the counter, stirring a cup of coffee that had long gone cold. His brows furrowed as he read the newspaper, his glasses sliding down his nose. Julia hesitated before stepping closer, twisting the rag in her hands.

"Got a minute?" she asked softly.

Charles glanced up, immediately noticing the tension in her face. He folded the newspaper and gestured to the stool beside him. "Always."

She sat down, exhaling shakily. Her fingers traced the edge of the counter as she searched for the right words.

"I'm leaving," she said finally.

Charles's expression shifted—surprise first, then something deeper, something close to relief. "Leaving your husband?"

She nodded. "In a couple of weeks. While he's at work."

Charles set his coffee down, his eyes scanning her face like he was searching for signs of hesitation. "Are you sure about this?"

"Yes." Her voice was stronger than she expected. "I can't stay. Not after…" She trailed off, unwilling to give voice to the nightmare of the other night. She rubbed her wrist, the bruised skin a stark reminder of why this had to happen.

Charles noticed the motion, his jaw tightening. "Where are you going?"

"My cousin Rick lives in Kentucky. He manages a mobile home park and has a place for me and Sarah. Ed wouldn't think to look there."

Charles nodded slowly, taking it all in. "You got enough money to get there?"

Julia hesitated before shaking her head. "Enough for gas, maybe a little food. But after that…"

He reached into his pocket and pulled out his wallet without hesitation. "Take this." He slid a few folded bills across the counter.

She stared at the money, shaking her head. "Charles, I can't—"

"Yes, you can," he interrupted. "It's not charity, Julia. It's a friend making sure you and your little girl are safe."

Her throat tightened. She wanted to argue, but the truth was, she needed it. And the kindness in Charles's eyes—the quiet, unwavering support—made it impossible to refuse.

With a trembling hand, she picked up the money and tucked it into her apron. "Thank you." Her voice cracked.

Charles reached out, his fingers lightly brushing over her bruised wrist. His expression darkened. "If he ever comes near you again, you tell me. I don't care how far away you are."

A tear slipped down her cheek, but this time, it wasn't from fear. It was from something dangerously close to *hope*.

"I'll be okay," she whispered.

Charles studied her for a long moment before nodding. "Yeah, you will."

**

A Gift of Faith

A few days had passed since Julia confided in Charles about leaving Ed. She had been meticulous in her preparations—carefully tucking away cash, making plans with Rick, ensuring Sarah's things could be packed in a single duffel bag. Each day brought her closer to freedom, but also closer to fear.

What if something went wrong? What if Ed found out? What if she was making a mistake?

The thoughts weighed heavily on her as she stood outside the diner, the cool evening air biting at her skin. Her shift had just ended, and she had stepped out for a breath of fresh air before heading home. The last place she wanted to go.

She startled slightly when Charles's voice cut through the quiet. "You alright?"

She turned to see him standing beside her, hands in the pockets of his worn jacket. His gaze was steady, concerned.

"I don't know," she admitted. "Some days, I feel ready. Other days, I feel like I'm about to step off a cliff with no idea if I'll land on my feet."

Charles nodded, as if he understood that feeling all too well. "Got something for you," he said, pulling a small object from his pocket. He handed her a tiny box, no bigger than a matchbook.

Curious, Julia opened it, revealing a single mustard seed resting against the dark velvet lining. She looked up at him, puzzled.

"It's from my grandmother," Charles explained. "She used to say if you have faith even as small as a mustard seed, you can move mountains. You don't have to see the whole path, Julia. You just have to take the first step."

Julia swallowed hard, her fingers brushing over the tiny seed. Something about its simplicity, its smallness, made her chest ache. It was a reminder that even the smallest *hope*, the tiniest belief in herself, was enough.

"I don't know if I have that kind of faith," she whispered.

Charles tilted his head slightly. "You do. You're here, aren't you? Planning, fighting for something better. That's faith."

She let out a shaky breath, closing the box gently. "Thank you, Charles. For this… for everything."

"You don't owe me thanks," he said softly. "Just promise me you'll keep going. And keep drawing."

At the mention of her art, a faint smile touched her lips. "You really think I can do something with it?"

He held her gaze. "I know you can."

For the first time in a long time, Julia felt something stir inside her that wasn't fear or doubt. It was small, fragile—but it was there.

Hope.

She clenched the little box in her palm, letting it anchor her.

She was ready to take the first step.

**

A Sketch of Hope

That night, after tucking Sarah in, Julia tiptoed into the bedroom, bracing herself for whatever mood Ed might be in. But as she peeked inside, relief washed over her—he was already asleep, his heavy, rhythmic breathing filling the darkened room. She hesitated in the doorway, her eyes lingering on the man who had controlled her for so long. The sight of him no longer stirred affection or regret. Just a quiet, exhausted resignation.

She backed out of the room as silently as she had entered, closing the door behind her before slipping into the small living room. The air in the house was thick, heavy with the weight of to many unspoken words and hidden bruises. But tonight, it felt different. The little box Charles had given her was still clutched in her hand, the tiny mustard seed a quiet reminder that change was possible.

With careful hands, she set it on the coffee table and reached for her bag. The moment she pulled out her sketchpad, a wave of nervous energy pulsed through her. It had been so long since she had drawn just for herself. Since she had allowed herself to create without guilt or fear.

She flipped to a blank page, the paper crisp beneath her fingertips. Then, gripping the pencil, she let her hand move freely, following the pull of something deep inside her. Lines emerged, soft and tentative at first, then growing bolder. She didn't have a clear vision at the start, but as she worked, it began to take shape—Sarah's face, peaceful and full of innocence, her little hands reaching for something unseen.

But it wasn't just Sarah. In the background, Julia found herself sketching something unexpected—a woman standing just behind the child. She was only half-formed, as if she were emerging from shadows, but there was something unmistakable in her stance. Strength. Determination. A quiet but unyielding resilience.

Julia stared at the drawing, her heart thudding in her chest. It was her.

Or at least, the woman she hoped to become.

Her fingers trembled as she set the pencil down. She traced the lines of her own image, marveling at the quiet power in the figure's posture. Was this really inside her? This strength, this possibility?

She glanced at the tiny box on the table, then back at the drawing.

Maybe faith wasn't about being certain. Maybe it was simply about believing enough to take the next step.

And she was ready.

With a deep breath, Julia closed the sketchpad and held it to her chest. In just a few weeks, she would be gone. Far from this house, far from Ed. And for the first time in years, she wouldn't just be surviving.

She would be living.

**

Another Evening at the Diner

The evening rush had passed, leaving the diner bathed in the soft glow of overhead lights. The scent of coffee lingered in the air, mingling with the faint sounds of conversation from the few remaining customers. Julia moved through the space with practiced ease, clearing plates and refilling cups, but her mind was elsewhere.

Charles was still at his usual booth, nursing the last of his coffee. He had been watching her in that quiet, observant way he always did—not intrusive, not demanding, just… present. It made her both comforted and nervous all at once.

She hesitated before approaching, pressing the rag she was holding into her apron pocket. "Need a warm-up?" she asked, nodding toward his cup.

He glanced down at it, then back at her with a small smile. "Nah. Just thinking."

Julia slid into the seat across from him without really meaning to. Maybe it was exhaustion, or maybe it was something else—some unspoken pull between them that had only grown stronger over the last few weeks.

"What about?" she asked, folding her hands in her lap.

Charles studied her for a long moment before exhaling through his nose, shaking his head slightly. "You."

Her breath hitched, but she forced herself to keep steady. "Me?"

He leaned forward, resting his forearms on the table. "I know you've got a plan. I know you're set on leaving, and that's good. You need to. But I just…" He let out a slow breath, rubbing the back of his neck. "I don't want this to be the last time we talk."

Something warm and unfamiliar stirred in her chest. "I told you I'd keep in touch."

"I know," he said, his voice softer now. "And I believe you. But I guess what I'm trying to say is… I don't just want to hear that you're okay. I want to hear your voice. I want to know how you're really doing. I want to…" He hesitated, then sighed. "I want to keep knowing you, Julia."

Her heart pounded in her chest.

She had known—on some level, she had known—that Charles saw her as more than just a woman in a bad situation. But hearing it out loud, seeing the way his fingers fidgeted slightly as he spoke, as if he wasn't sure how she'd respond, made it real in a way that both scared and thrilled her.

"I don't know what life's going to look like once I leave," she admitted, her voice barely above a whisper. "I don't even know if I'll have time to think about—" She cut herself off, shaking her head.

"Me?" Charles finished for her, a knowing smile tugging at the corner of his mouth.

She swallowed hard. "I just need to focus on Sarah and getting settled."

"I know," he said again. "And I'd never ask you for anything more than you're ready to give." He reached across the table then, his fingers grazing hers. It wasn't a grand gesture, wasn't anything anyone else in the diner would even notice. But Julia felt it everywhere.

"I just want you to know," he continued, his thumb brushing lightly against her knuckles before he pulled away. "That whenever you are ready—whether it's a month from now, a year, or never—I'll be here."

Julia exhaled slowly, feeling something shift inside her.

For years, she had convinced herself that love was an obligation, that relationships were about endurance rather than choice. But here was a man telling her she had a choice. That she had time. That she was worth waiting for.

She glanced down at her lap, then back up at him. "Thank you," she murmured, her fingers still tingling where he had touched them.

He gave her a slow, steady nod. "Take care of yourself, Julia."

And for the first time in a long, long time, she thought maybe—just maybe—she would.

**

A Conversation Left Unspoken

Julia sat at the kitchen table, her fingers wrapped around a mug of lukewarm coffee, staring at the familiar lines of her mother's face. Anne moved around the kitchen with practiced efficiency, wiping the already clean counters, adjusting the ceramic canisters on the shelf—anything to keep busy.

Julia swallowed hard. The words sat heavy in her chest, pressing against her ribs, aching to come out. She had rehearsed them over and over in her mind: Mama, I'm leaving Ed. I'm taking Sarah, and we're going to Kentucky. I need you to understand.

But now, sitting here in the house she grew up in, under her mother's sharp, watchful eyes, the words refused to come.

Anne finally sat across from her, folding her hands neatly on the table. "You're awfully quiet today," she remarked, her tone light but laced with scrutiny. "Something on your mind?"

Julia's pulse quickened. This was it—her chance. She could tell her mother everything. The bruises. The fear. The plan.

She opened her mouth.

Then she saw it—the way Anne's lips were already pressed together in that disapproving line, the way her gaze held the weight of judgment before Julia had even spoken.

Julia knew exactly how this conversation would go. Anne would shake her head, sigh like Julia was a foolish little girl, and say something like, Marriage isn't easy, Julia. You don't just walk away because it gets hard.

Maybe she'd remind her how her own father had his "bad days," how Anne had stuck it out because that's what a wife does. Maybe she'd talk about Sarah and how she needed both her parents, needed stability.

Maybe she'd even say, You made your bed, Julia.

The words swelled in her throat, then died before they could escape.

Instead, she forced a small smile. "Just tired," she said quietly, taking a sip of her coffee to avoid her mother's eyes.

Anne nodded knowingly, as if she had been expecting that answer. "That's no surprise. Taking care of a home, a husband, a little girl—it's a lot of work. But that's life, honey."

Julia only nodded, her hands tightening around the mug.

She wouldn't tell her. There was no point.

When she left, when she was far away, her mother would hear about it eventually. And when she did, Julia already knew exactly what she would say.

I raised you better than this.

So she sat in silence, letting the moment slip away, pretending—just for now—that everything was fine.

**

A Moment Alone

Julia sat in her car outside her mother's house, gripping the steering wheel so tightly her knuckles turned white. The lump in her throat wouldn't go away, no matter how many deep breaths she took. The words she had wanted to say still sat there, heavy and unspoken, like stones weighing her down.

She had known it would be like this. She had known she wouldn't be able to get through to her mother. And yet, the disappointment still stung.

Why did I even try?

Her mother's voice still echoed in her ears—soft but firm, laced with that same unwavering belief that a woman's duty was to endure. To accept. To hold a family together, no matter the cost to herself.

A sharp ache spread through her chest as she thought of all the times she had sought comfort here, hoping for understanding but always walking away with the same empty feeling.

She stared at the dashboard, her vision blurring with unshed tears. What if I'm wrong? What if I'm making a mistake?

The doubt crept in like a slow-moving tide, threatening to drown her resolve. Her mother had made it work. So had so many other women before her. Maybe she just wasn't strong enough. Maybe she hadn't tried hard enough.

But then she thought of Sarah. Of the way her daughter's small body tensed whenever Ed raised his voice. Of the way she clung to Julia when things got bad, whispering, Mama, let's just be quiet, okay? as if their silence could protect them.

Julia shut her eyes tightly. No. This wasn't just about her anymore.

Her mother didn't have to understand.

Her mother didn't have to approve.

She was leaving anyway.

A slow breath trembled out of her as she opened her eyes and turned the key in the ignition. The engine rumbled to life, a steady, solid sound that grounded her.

She wiped her cheeks quickly before shifting into gear.

There was still so much to do. But for the first time since she had started planning her escape, she realized something important.

She didn't need her mother's blessing.

She only needed the strength to keep going.

And she had that.

She had that.

Julia went back to the diner for just a few more minutes to clear her head before going home for the evening. There sat Charles at a corner table. Odd time for him to be here she thought. She wondered if he came in more than she knew. Charles had a tablet and pencil in front of him. He laid down the pencil as she approached him. “Hey, I never expected to see you here.” He motioned for her to take a seat across from him. "Sure".

“What are you doing here this evening Julia?”

“Oh just taking another breath before heading home”

“Oh, I figured you were already home”

“Nah, I just came from my mothers. I tried to tell her about the thoughts I've been having about leaving Ed but I just couldn't. I know she won't approve, but I've also decided that I don't need her approval to make my decision to be safe and keep my daughter safe.”

“ Yeah, I bet that's a tough one. You and your mom seem to be close.”

“Yes, we usually are, but we differ on this topic. Although, I haven't told her all the details of what's really going on in our house. Perhaps she would be more understanding if I did. She likes Ed though, so I don't feel right making him seem like a bad guy.”

"Really, Julia, he's a bad guy. Why do you feel the need to protect him by not sharing with your mom? I have a feeling that if she knew the details of how he treats you, she would not be pushing you to stay with him."

That hit Julia hard. She knew Charles was right, but the weight of her mother's expectations still clung to her like a heavy chain. She let out a slow breath and rubbed her sore wrist absentmindedly. "I guess part of me just wants to believe that if I don't say it out loud, it's not as bad as it really is."

Charles studied her, his expression both gentle and firm. "But it is that bad, Julia. And you deserve better."

She nodded, looking away for a moment. "I know."

He tapped the side of his tablet, drawing her attention back. "You know, sometimes when things get too tangled up in my head, I draw. Helps me sort things out." He turned the tablet toward her, and her breath caught.

It was a sketch of her—soft lines, delicate shading, but unmistakably her. She was looking off to the side, thoughtful, with a quiet strength in her eyes that she wasn't sure she actually possessed.

"You drew this?" she asked, her voice barely above a whisper.

He gave a small, almost shy nod. "Yeah. I guess I've been seeing you a lot lately."

A warmth spread through her chest, unfamiliar yet not unwelcome. "It's beautiful."

Charles gave her a small smile, but then his expression turned serious. "I mean it, Julia. You're strong. You just have to see it the way I do."

She swallowed hard, touched more than she knew how to express.

"I also meant what I said before," he continued, holding her gaze. "I want to keep in touch. When you leave for Kentucky, I don't want that to be the end of… whatever this is."

Julia hesitated, emotions swirling inside her. "Charles…"

"You don't have to promise anything," he said quickly, leaning forward. "I just want you to know I care about what happens to you. And I hope you'll let me be part of your life, even if it's from a distance."

She looked down at her hands, then back up at him. "I'd like that," she admitted.

His smile was small, but it lit up his eyes. "Good."

For the first time in a long time, Julia felt like someone truly saw her—not just as a wife or a mother, but as a person who mattered.

Julia points to the tablet and the sketch, so you draw too? You never mentioned that. Oh yeah, I do. If you wanna know the details, I do more than sketch. What, what do you mean? Charles, not wanting to seem to pompous, looked at her in a soft, almost shy way, "I paint too and I teach classes at the local college. "Wow, I had no idea Julia said as she admired the sketch he drew of her. So that's why you noticed my doodles. She said with a small grin.

Charles chuckled, rubbing the back of his neck. "Yeah, I guess you could say I have an eye for it. But your 'doodles' are more than just scribbles, Julia. You've got real talent."

Julia glanced down at the sketch on his tablet, her lips parting slightly in surprise. It was her—soft lines capturing the curve of her face, the depth in her eyes, the quiet strength she never thought anyone noticed.

"I—I don't know what to say," she murmured, tracing a fingertip near the edge of the drawing but not quite touching it. "You drew me?"

Charles nodded. "I guess I just wanted to capture you the way I see you." His voice was gentle, his gaze steady but uncertain, as if afraid he'd said too much.

Julia swallowed hard, emotions tightening her throat. No one had ever really looked at her like this, let alone taken the time to immortalize her in a piece of art. "It's beautiful," she whispered.

"So are you," he said quietly, almost like he hadn't meant to say it out loud.

Their eyes met, and for a moment, the world outside the booth faded. Julia's heart pounded, not just from the compliment, but from the way he saw her—like she was someone worth seeing. Someone worth cherishing.

But before she could speak, before she could even process the warmth blooming in her chest, Charles cleared his throat and glanced away, breaking the spell. "Anyway," he said, shifting in his seat, "I wanted to say… When you leave for Kentucky, I'd really like to keep in touch. If you'd like that, too."

Julia hesitated for only a second before nodding. "Yeah. I'd like that."

She knew she was walking a fine line, but for the first time in years, she felt like she wasn't walking it alone.

Julia glanced at the clock on the diner wall, and a quiet resolve settled over her. "I should get going," she said softly, rising from her seat.

Charles looked up, his expression gentle yet wistful. "Alright," he replied, his voice low. "Take care, Julia."

She offered him a small smile, her heart pounding with a mix of hope and uncertainty. As she walked toward the door, she felt his steady gaze follow her—a silent promise that she wasn't alone in this.

Stepping out into the cool night air, Julia clutched the tiny mustard seed that Charles had given her earlier—a symbol of faith and the fragile *hope* that had taken root in her heart. Her steps felt lighter, each one carrying her a little further from the life she was leaving behind, and a little closer to the future she was beginning to imagine.

**

In the Weeks That Followed

During the next few weeks, Julia endured more slaps and belittling words. Each harsh strike and every cruel remark tore at her, yet she bore them with a silent determination. Every act of abuse, every degrading word, served as a grim reminder of the life she was desperate to escape. She clung to the belief that before long she would be free from Ed and all of this horror.

Each day, despite the pain and humiliation, she meticulously prepared for the future she envisioned. In the quiet moments when Ed's rage had subsided, she would pull out her secret notebook and update her escape plan. Her heart pounded with both fear and hope as she imagined a new place—one where she could start over, build a new life, and shield Sarah from the cruelty that had defined their home.

She pictured a modest apartment or a small house where she and Sarah could live in peace. She dreamed of finding a job that respected her talents, perhaps something that would let her explore her artistic gifts—a future where her daughter would never have to see the harshness of Ed's world. The thought of Sarah's innocent laughter filling a warm, safe space was the light that carried her through the darkest hours.

Even on the hardest days, when each slap stung more than the last and the words cut deeper than any physical wound, Julia reminded herself that every moment of suffering was a step closer to freedom. Every bruised wrist, every tear shed in silence, was a testament to her resilience. She was determined that one day, she and Sarah would leave behind the cruelty of Ed for a life defined by love, stability, and hope.

And so, with each passing day, as she nursed her wounds and endured the abuse, Julia nurtured the promise of a new beginning—a promise that one day, she would finally be free.

**

That day had finally arrived.

The morning light filtered through the thin curtains, casting a soft glow across the bedroom as Julia quietly pulled a small suitcase from the closet. She had been awake for hours, staring at the ceiling, running through every step in her mind. Now, with Ed gone to work, it was time.

She moved quickly but carefully, pulling out enough clothes for both her and Sarah to last for a while. Just the essentials—no more than she could carry in the trunk of her car. A few of Sarah's favorite outfits, her stuffed rabbit, and the well-worn story book they read together every night. Julia took a deep breath and reached into the nightstand, retrieving a small envelope of cash she had been quietly saving, tucking it safely into her purse.

As she zipped up the suitcase, Sarah appeared in the doorway, rubbing the sleep from her eyes. "Mommy, what are you doing?"

Julia turned, forcing a soft smile. "We're going on a little trip, sweetheart."

Sarah frowned, her small brows knitting together. "A trip? But what about Daddy?"

Julia crouched down, brushing a stray curl from her daughter's face. "Daddy's staying here, honey. But you and I are going somewhere safe, somewhere special. It'll just be us for a little while."

Sarah's lip trembled, confusion swimming in her big eyes. "Did Daddy do something bad?"

Julia hesitated, choosing her words carefully. "Sometimes people change, baby. And sometimes, we have to make a new start."

Sarah looked down at the stuffed rabbit in her arms, hugging it tightly. "Will I still have my toys?"

Julia kissed the top of her head. "Of course. I packed your favorites."

She straightened, grabbing the suitcase handle and taking one last glance around the bedroom. It didn't feel like home anymore—it hadn't in a long time.

Taking Sarah's hand, she led her to the door. There was no turning back now.

**

A Final Farewell at the Diner

Before her long drive to Kentucky, Julia knew there was one more place that held the echoes of her past—one more final farewell visit when the diner was quiet and nearly empty. As she stepped inside with a determined heaviness in her heart, the scent of fresh coffee and sizzling bacon filled the air, wrapping around her like a bittersweet farewell. She held Sarah's tiny hand in hers, leading her toward the counter.

Sliding her onto a stool, she smiled down at her daughter. "How about chocolate milk and a cookie, sweetheart?"

Sarah beamed and nodded eagerly. Julia placed the order, her voice steady despite the weight in her chest. As she turned, her eyes met Charles'.

At a corner table near the window he sat, he gazed at his phone as he sipped his coffee. He looked up as Julia approached, his face softening into a warm, familiar smile.

"Julia," he greeted, his tone gentle and sincere, as though they were old friends meeting on a quiet morning rather than two people with a shared secret.

"Sit right here honey, mommy's going to go speak to a friend just over there for a second." Pointing in the direction of Charles.

"O.k. mommy."

She pulled out a chair and sat down, carefully tucking the tiny box with the mustard seed—Charles's gift—into her lap. "I had to come by one last time," she said quietly. "I wanted to say goodbye before I leave."

Charles's eyes flickered with concern. "Goodbye? I thought you might be coming back here to visit. Are you really leaving for good?"

Julia nodded, her throat tight. "Yes. I'm taking Sarah and heading to Kentucky. My cousin Rick has a trailer waiting for us there. I need a fresh start—a chance to build a life where we're safe."

He leaned forward, his gaze earnest. "I'm really glad you've found the strength to do this, Julia. I always believed you deserved more than the life you had here. I know it wasn't easy."

Her eyes shimmered as she reached out to gently squeeze his hand. "Thank you, Charles. Your kindness and support have meant more to me than I can say. You helped me see that I'm not alone—that I can believe in a better future."

Charles's smile was tender. "Promise me you'll take care of yourself—and Sarah, please keep in touch. I'd really like to hear about your new life in Kentucky. I want to know you're safe, and that you're finding the happiness you deserve."

She hesitated, then nodded, her voice steady despite the emotions swirling inside her. "I promise. I won't forget what you've done for me, or what you've given me." Her fingers brushed over the tiny mustard seed in the box, its presence a quiet beacon of hope.

For a long moment, they sat in companionable silence. The soft hum of the diner and the gentle morning light created a cocoon around them—a moment of tenderness and understanding before the inevitable goodbye.

Finally, Julia stood. "I should be going now," she said, her eyes meeting his with a mixture of gratitude and lingering sorrow.

Charles rose with her, and they shared one last look—a silent promise that their friendship would endure despite the miles that would soon separate them. "Take care, Julia. And remember, even the smallest seed can grow into something mighty," he said softly.

Stepping out into the cool morning air, Julia carried that thought—and that tiny mustard seed—in her heart. As she walked toward her car, her steps were filled with both the pain of farewell and the promise of a new beginning, a future where hope and courage would guide every step.

**

Chapter 2

The Road to Hopetown

Julia eased her car onto the open road, the early morning light giving way to a pale, promising day. As the familiar scenery blurred into the unknown, her mind wandered with a mixture of relief, trepidation, and an undeniable spark of *hope.* Every mile she put between herself and the old life felt like shedding another layer of pain.

Her thoughts drifted back to the final moments at the diner—the gentle encouragement in Charles's eyes, the soft warmth of his parting words, and the tiny mustard seed that now lay secure in her pocket. It was a symbol, small yet mighty, reminding her that even the tiniest seed of faith could blossom into something magnificent.

As she drove, the rhythmic hum of the engine became a steady heartbeat, accompanying her reflections. What if this is the beginning of everything I've dreamed of? she wondered, her hands steady on the wheel despite the storm of emotions within. The road stretched out before her like a promise—long, winding, and uncertain—but it was hers to travel.

In the rearview mirror, she saw the fading outline of her old life—a house once filled with memories of abuse, a town that had known too much sorrow. Ahead, the horizon glowed with the possibility of change. *I'm doing this for Sarah and for me,* she reminded herself firmly. *I deserve to be safe, to be happy.*

The landscape changed gradually. Urban sprawl gave way to open fields, and eventually, she caught sight of a sign that read, "Welcome to ***Hopetown***." The quaint name brought a small, hopeful smile to her lips. ***Hopetown***—a place that sounded as if it were made for new beginnings, where the echoes of the past could finally be left behind and replaced with fresh starts.

With each mile, the fear and uncertainty that had once paralyzed her receded, replaced by a cautious optimism. The car's steady pace gave her time to ponder the practicalities of her escape—the new home in ***Hopetown***, the fresh start at a job where she could rebuild her life, and the opportunity to pursue her art freely, without the constant shadow of Ed's cruelty.

Yet, the road was not without its echoes of doubt. At times, a sharp pang of loneliness and anxiety reminded her of the challenges ahead. What if she stumbled along the way? What if the past caught up to her? But then she would feel the smooth, reassuring shape of the tiny mustard seed in her pocket, and she would remember Charles's words: even a small seed of faith can move mountains.

The car's headlights illuminated the dark stretches ahead as dusk began to fall, but within her, a small light burned steadily. ***Hopetown*** was more than just a destination—it was a promise of a future where every step, no matter how tentative, was a step away from pain and toward a life of hope, safety, and renewal.

As Julia navigated the quiet, winding roads, she whispered to herself, "I'm almost there. I'm free." And with that, she pressed on, determined to embrace the new dawn that awaited in ***Hopetown***

**

Arrival at Rick's

The road led Julia through gentle hills and fields bathed in the soft glow of twilight. As she turned onto a narrow lane marked "Mobile Home Park," a sense of both relief and trepidation settled over her. The faded sign read simply, "Rick's Park." In that quiet moment, Julia realized this was the threshold of a new beginning.

She parked her old sedan under a large oak, its leaves whispering in the cool evening breeze, and stepped out. The park was serene—rows of modest trailers and well-kept lawns arranged along winding paths. A modest building with a weathered sign reading "Office" stood at the entrance, offering a subtle promise of order amidst change.

Before Julia could gather her swirling thoughts, a pickup truck pulled up beside her. The door swung open, and Rick emerged—a man whose kind eyes and lined face spoke of years spent caring for family and community. When he saw her, his expression softened into a warm smile that felt both welcoming and reassuring.

"Julia," Rick said in a steady, gentle tone, "it's good to see you. And who's this?" He crouched down to greet the little girl peeking shyly from behind her mother.

"This is Sarah," Julia replied, her voice barely concealing the mix of exhaustion and hope in her tone. "I'm here… I'm really here, Rick."

Rick extended his arms, pulling both mother and daughter into a comforting embrace. "You're always welcome here. I've got a unit ready for you, just as we talked about."

He led them along a quiet path toward the office building. The park felt like a world away from the chaos Julia had left behind. The air smelled of freshly cut grass, and somewhere nearby, the gentle sound of children laughing drifted on the wind.

Inside the small office, Rick motioned for Julia to come closer. On a cluttered desk lay a set of keys, their metallic glint promising a safe haven. "This trailer is yours," he said. "It's modest, but it's secure, and you can make it your own home."

Julia accepted the keys with trembling hands, overwhelmed by a mixture of relief and the gravity of the new start ahead. "Thank you, Rick," she managed. "You don't know how much this means to us."

Rick's gaze softened further as he spoke quietly, "Family takes care of family, Julia. I know you've been through a lot, and I promise you, things will be different here. You deserve happiness."

Outside again, under the vast Kentucky sky, Sarah's small hand slipped into Julia's. Looking at her daughter, Julia felt an inner strength stirring—an affirmation that every painful step taken was leading them both toward safety and renewal.

In that moment, surrounded by the quiet of the mobile home park and the genuine care in Rick's eyes, Julia allowed herself to believe in the possibility of a better future. A future where *hope*, fragile yet persistent as a mustard seed, could finally grow into something strong and enduring.

**

Settling In

Julia parked her car in the small, uneven lot of the mobile home and stepped out into the quiet Kentucky evening. The soft glow of the moon mingled with the warm light of a safety lamp on a nearby post, casting gentle shadows over the trailer and welcoming them into a haven of safety and new beginnings.

Hand in hand with Sarah, Julia carefully unloaded her few possessions from the car. Sarah clutched her beloved ragged bunny and a small, well-worn blanket that she always snuggled with at night. Each item they carried felt both precious and heavy—a testament to a past they were leaving behind and a future they were eager to embrace.

Inside the trailer, the space was sparse but clean, the air smelled faintly of fresh paint. Julia set her battered duffel bag down in the narrow hallway and began arranging the few linens on the old, worn mattress. As she carefully tucked a faded quilt over the bed, she paused to smooth out creases—each fold symbolizing a small act of rebuilding a life free from the fragments of the past.

In the living area, Sarah sat on the floor with her blanket wrapped around her, holding her bunny close. Her wide eyes took in every new detail of the modest space, and for a moment, she whispered, "It feels like a new home, Mama." Julia smiled gently, wrapping an arm around Sarah, reassuring her that yes—it was a beginning.

As the evening deepened into night, Julia stepped back to survey the room. The few belongings they had brought whispered of memories and dreams—of moments that had defined their past, and of *hopes* that were just beginning to take shape. Outside, the crickets began their nightly chorus, and the soft light from the moon and the safety lamp merged to create a serene glow that filled the trailer with gentle promise.

Julia sat on the edge of the bed, with Sarah snuggled against her, the little bunny tucked under Sarah's arm and the blanket draped over both of them. In that quiet stillness, every bruise, every tear, every painful memory seemed to fade away, replaced by the tender certainty of a new beginning.

This was not just a temporary refuge—it was the first step toward a future where she and Sarah could finally feel safe. With each careful placement of their meager possessions, Julia was building more than just a home. She was rebuilding her identity, reclaiming her hope, and carving out a space where love and resilience could flourish.

As she listened to the gentle hum of the night, with Sarah's soft breaths mingling with the whisper of the wind outside, Julia allowed herself to believe that in this small, humble trailer, a better life was finally within reach.

**

New Beginnings

The morning sun filtered through the trees outside Rick's modest office building, casting shadows over the mobile home park. Julia had spent the previous night sorting her belongings and quietly planning the next steps of her life. Today, she knew, was about more than just a new house—it was about rebuilding everything she had lost.

She found Rick in his small office, surrounded by papers and a well-worn desk that bore the marks of years of hard work. Rick looked up as she and Sarah entered, offering a warm, fatherly smile.

"Morning, young ladies. How are you holding up Julia?" he asked, his tone gentle but laced with concern.

Julia took a steadying breath before replying, "I'm... managing, Rick. It's still a lot to take in, but I'm trying to make a start." Her eyes drifted to the floor for a moment, then back to him. "I need to talk about work—and about finding a safe way to care for Sarah while I get things in order."

Rick leaned back, folding his hands on the desk. "Work's important. What are you thinking? I know you've got a lot of talent, not just in art but in all the skills you developed over the years."

She managed a small smile. "I was wondering if you might know of any openings around here. Something steady. And maybe, if possible, a babysitting service or a childcare arrangement that I can trust until I get back on my feet. I can't risk leaving Sarah alone with just anyone."

Rick nodded thoughtfully. "I might be able to help with that. Over the years, I've seen a lot of folks in our community struggle with the same issues. There's a local non-profit that runs a childcare cooperative—it's designed for people who need a safe, affordable place for their kids while they work. I've heard good things about it." He paused, then added, "I can introduce you to someone there, if you'd like, or there's Teresa who lives here in the park, she watches other children.

Julia's eyes brightened just a little. "That would be amazing, Rick. I need a job that's steady, and a reliable place for Sarah. I can't risk her safety, not after everything."

Rick smiled gently. "I know it's been hard, Julia. And I know starting over isn't easy. But you have strength—and you're not alone in this. I'll do whatever I can to help you get established here." He paused, leaning forward. "I might even have a few leads at some local businesses looking for someone with your skills. I'll ask around. But first, let's get you set up with childcare. Safety for Sarah is the most important thing."

Julia felt a surge of gratitude as she nodded. "Thank you, Rick. I… I really appreciate it. I want to make a better life for Sarah and for me. I know it's not going to be easy, but I have to try."

Rick reached across the desk and squeezed her hand reassuringly. "You're already taking the right steps. We'll get through this together. Remember, family takes care of family, and I'm here to help you every step of the way."

In that small, cluttered office filled with the promise of new beginnings, Julia felt a tentative spark of hope. With Rick's support, the prospect of finding steady work and a safe childcare solution for Sarah no longer seemed like a distant dream. It was a concrete plan—a foundation upon which she could finally rebuild her life.

As they continued to talk, mapping out the next steps of her journey, Julia realized that while the road ahead was still uncertain, she was no longer walking it alone. And that, in itself, was a reason to believe in the future she was starting to create.

Rick leaned forward, tapping his pen lightly on the desk. "So, Julia, what kind of work do you see yourself doing?" he asked, his tone warm yet curious.

Julia hesitated before replying softly, "I know I've done office work before, but I really love drawing—and something to do with that I would love. I'd like to have some creative time, but right now, I need something steady. I need a Monday-to-Friday job that pays the bills while I figure out how to focus on art part-time."

Rick nodded thoughtfully. "That makes sense. You need stability to get started, especially with Sarah. There are a few options that might work for you—a role that's steady enough, yet leaves you some space for creativity on the side."

Julia's eyes brightened slightly. "What do you have in mind?"

"Well," Rick began, "there's a local administrative job at the community center. It's a Monday-to-Friday position, and while it's not an art job per se, it would give you a consistent income and some regular hours. Plus, the community center often has events where your creative touch might come in handy—like putting together flyers or helping with layouts for their newsletters."

Julia considered this, nodding slowly. "That could work. It wouldn't be ideal, but it's something steady until I can transition into more art-related work."

Rick smiled. "Exactly. It's a way to keep the lights on, build up a little savings, and not feel completely boxed in. Once you're more secure, you can take on freelance projects or even pursue teaching art classes if that's what you'd like."

She let out a sigh, a mix of relief and cautious optimism. "I need that stability for Sarah and for myself. I want to eventually focus on art, but I can't do that until I know we're safe."

Rick's eyes softened with understanding. "I know, Julia. We'll figure it out together. I can introduce you to someone at the community center. They're always looking for reliable people, and I think you'd be a great fit. It'll give you the chance to work regular hours, and who knows—you might find that even in an office setting, there's room for your creative spark."

Julia managed a small, hopeful smile. "Thank you, Rick. It means a lot to know that I have options that let me be both secure and true to myself."

Rick reached across the desk, giving her hand a reassuring squeeze. "You deserve that balance, Julia. I'll set up a meeting for you. In the meantime, focus on what you need to do to get started. We'll take it one step at a time."

Their conversation tapered into a quiet understanding, the weight of practical concerns mingling with the spark of a new beginning. Although the details were still unfolding, Julia felt reassured. With a steady job on the horizon to support her and Sarah, she could gradually carve out the space to nurture her art and rebuild her life.

**

Chapter 3

The Reckoning

Ed's fury boiled over as he stormed into the diner, his eyes wild and searching for a ghost that wasn't there. The usual murmur of late-night customers fell silent as he banged his way through the entrance, his voice booming through the room.

"Where is she? Where is my wife?" he roared, scanning every face as if expecting to find Julia among them.

The diner's few patrons shrank back in alarm, their conversations ceasing under the weight of his anger. At a corner table, Charles looked up from his tablet, his eyes narrowing with concern and determination. The familiar calm he usually exuded was replaced by a steely resolve.

"Ed, enough," Charles said firmly, rising from his seat and stepping toward him. "You're not welcome here making a scene."

Ed's eyes flared with indignation as he faced Charles. "And who are you to tell me what I can or cannot do? This is my family, and I demand to know where she is!"

Charles's tone remained unwavering. "Julia made her choice. You've hurt her, and she's taken her daughter and left. If you're here to cause trouble, you need to leave now."

A murmur rippled through the diner as Ed's voice cracked with a mixture of anger and desperation. "I have every right to find her! I won't let her just walk away from what we built."

Charles stepped closer, his presence calm but unyielding. "What you built wasn't love—it was control and pain. Julia's gone, Ed. And until you learn to control your anger, until you understand that she won't come back to this cruelty, you're not going to find her here."

Ed's face contorted, a snarl twisting his features. For a long, tense moment, neither spoke, the silence charged with the inevitable fallout of their confrontation. The few remaining customers exchanged uneasy glances, the air heavy with unspoken judgment.

Finally, with one last glare at Charles, Ed stormed out of the diner, his retreat punctuated by the sound of the door slamming shut behind him.

Charles stood alone in the aftermath, the quiet of the diner slowly returning. Though Julia was not there, his words had been spoken for her—an unyielding stand against the abuse that had driven her away. In that charged moment, it was clear: sometimes, the hardest battles are fought in the silence after the storm.

Charles sat in the lingering silence of the diner, his thoughts churning as he replayed the scene of Ed's outburst. In the quiet aftermath, a question weighed on him: Should he reach out to Julia and let her know that Ed now knew she had left, or should he let her savor this hard-won peace a little longer?

He recalled the sparkle in her eyes when she accepted the tiny mustard seed—a symbol of the faith and hope she was beginning to nurture. To shatter that calm with harsh news might be like pulling a thread from a fragile tapestry, risking unraveling the new life she was slowly stitching together.

She deserves this quiet space, Charles thought. She's fought so hard just to feel safe, to feel free—even if just for a moment. If I tell her now, she might be plunged back into fear and uncertainty, and I don't want to do that.

Yet, another part of him whispered that keeping her in the dark might be a disservice. What if she finds out later and feels betrayed by my silence? That thought made his heart tighten. But as he weighed the potential consequences, he realized that Julia's strength was still in its tender beginnings. Overwhelming her with the reality of Ed's realization might undo the progress she'd fought so hard to achieve.

He closed his eyes briefly, the low hum of the diner and a distant radio providing a backdrop to his inner debate. No, not now, he decided resolutely. She needs to remain in her newfound peace until she's ready to face the next step.

Charles resolved then that he would monitor the situation quietly. If he sensed that Julia was ready—if she reached out, or if her demeanor shifted—then he would gently bring the matter up. Until that moment arrived, he would keep her safe in silence, letting her continue to build her strength at her own pace.

With a final, quiet exhalation, Charles opened his tablet and began to type a message to himself—a reminder to check in on her later, but not to disturb the calm she had so desperately earned. In that moment, he vowed silently to be there for her with patience and unwavering support.

Ed slammed the diner door behind him, his heart pounding furiously as he raced to his car. The cool night air whipped at his face, but it did little to cool the blaze burning inside him. Seated behind the wheel, he gripped it tightly, his knuckles white with rage. The interior of the car was dimly lit by the dashboard, and in that half-light, his eyes burned with a mix of anger and bitter disbelief.

How could she do this? He seethed silently. How could she just walk away without a word? Each memory of their years together—of heated arguments, quiet reconciliations, and the painful moments of control—flashed before his eyes. Now, his pride and his delusions of ownership crumbled into bitter fragments.

His mind churned with a turbulent cocktail of emotions. Anger warred with humiliation as he replayed the scenes at the diner, the shame of being publicly rebuked gnawing at him. She thinks she can just escape me? he thought bitterly. She has no idea what she's giving up.

Yet, beneath the seething fury, a faint, unsettling whisper of regret began to surface—one that he quickly smothered with a clenched jaw. It wasn't a weakness, he told himself. It was a sign of failure. A failure to control what he believed was rightfully his. And that thought stoked the flames of his anger even further.

As he sat in the car, the rhythmic thrum of the engine became a metronome to his inner turmoil. He recalled the way Julia had looked that morning, the quiet determination in her eyes that now felt like a betrayal to his sense of control. Every slap, every harsh word they had exchanged seemed insignificant compared to the shock of her departure. Now, the silence in the car was oppressive—a reminder of the void she had left behind.

I must find her, he resolved, the idea growing more desperate with each passing second. The thought of searching, of chasing after the one person who had defied him, both infuriated and terrified him. But as much as he wanted to reclaim her, the reality of her absence—and his own failure to keep her in line—weighed on him like a leaden burden.

For a long, agonizing moment, Ed sat there, the neon reflections from the city outside flickering across his face. The anger in his chest was a constant, pulsing ache, and yet it was laced with uncertainty—a silent question that he refused to answer: Could he really live without her? Could he force her back to him?

The answer eluded him, swallowed by the roar of his own resentment. As he started the car and merged into the darkened street, Ed's thoughts remained a turbulent storm. The road ahead was uncertain, driven by a desperate need to regain control—even as he knew, deep down, that everything was slipping away.

In that car, Ed's internal monologue was a relentless barrage: accusations against Julia, denials of his own failings, and a growing, unsettling fear of the empty space she'd left behind. And with every mile, as the city lights faded into the distance, his anger grew more consuming—a dark promise that one day, he would force her to face the consequences of her choices.

But for now, the road stretched out before him, and with it, a future he could neither fully grasp nor control—a future that haunted him with the specter of loss and the bitter echo of a love turned sour.

**

The Search

Ed's fury simmered as he merged onto the dark highway, the neon lights of the city dissolving into the distance. His internal monologue was a chaotic mix of anger, desperation, and denial. The roar of the engine seemed to echo his racing thoughts: Where is she? How could she leave me? I must get her back.

Every passing mile deepened his resolve to reclaim control. He replayed the scene at the diner over and over in his head—the shame of being publicly rejected, the bitter taste of humiliation that still clung to him. Now, driving through the silence of the night, he was a man on a mission, determined to track down Julia at any cost.

Ed pulled into a nearly deserted gas station, his mind a whirlwind of tactics. He leaned over the fuel pump, tapping the side of the car with restless fingers, as he considered his next move. Maybe I should ask around—neighbors, coworkers, anyone who might have seen her. Someone must have noticed something. His voice was rough in his own mind, tinged with a mix of entitlement and wounded pride.

In the small convenience store attached to the station, he found himself stalled in a corner, glancing at the clock. His thoughts grew increasingly erratic as he recalled fragments of conversations he'd overheard while in the diner. A coworker had mentioned something about Julia missing work. Every piece of information, however small, became a vital clue in his desperate quest.

He pulled out his phone and made a few calls, his tone growing harsher with each unanswered ring. She can't have gone far, he muttered, frustration mounting with every silence on the other end. Each ring, each voicemail, only stoked the flames of his desperation further.

By the time he finally left the gas station, Ed's mind was a cluster of bitter thoughts. Every person he encountered seemed to blur together as he scanned the faces on the street, searching for a sign—a glimmer that might lead him to her. His heart pounded with a mix of rage and a disquieting hint of fear: What if I really lose her? What if I've already lost her?

Ed's desperation was no longer just about anger—it was about the gnawing terror of abandonment. That fear, though he would never admit it, was the root of his need to regain control. With each passing minute, he was driven by the need to find her, to force the reality of their separation to bend back in his favor.

As the night deepened and grew quieter, Ed pulled off the highway and drove through neighborhoods he suspected she might have visited. His eyes darted to every parked car, every flickering streetlight, searching, waiting for a sign that would lead him to Julia.

In the solitude of his car, his internal monologue echoed relentlessly: She's out there. I need to find her. I need to make her come back. And with every mile, the man who had once thought himself in control now felt the bitter pinch of loss, propelling him forward into a future defined by the chaos of his own making.

**

Chapter 4

A Mother's Shock and Concern

Anne sat in the dim light of the parlor, her gaze fixed on the silent telephone. The house, once filled with the comforting hum of conversation and the familiar sounds of family life, now felt oppressively quiet. As she sipped a cooling cup of tea, a deep, unsettling worry crept over her—a worry that perhaps things had been far worse between Julia and Ed than she had ever imagined.

She recalled the many evenings when she had urged Julia to persevere through marital struggles, convinced that every hardship could be overcome with time and sacrifice. But now, the stark reality of Julia's departure filled her with a raw, gnawing concern. What if I never truly knew the extent of their suffering? Anne wondered bitterly, her heart twisting with regret. Had I been so blinded by tradition and duty that I failed to see the depth of the abuse?

The memories of Julia's soft laughter from years past—when her daughter had been a bright, hopeful child with dreams unburdened by cruelty—now clashed with the painful image of a woman forced to leave her home, her spirit battered by Ed's harshness. Anne's thoughts were a tumult of sorrow and worry. She knew that Julia had made this choice not on a whim, but as a desperate bid for safety and freedom. Yet the pain of loss was tempered by a deep maternal instinct: the overwhelming need to protect her daughter.

Anne rose from her chair and walked to the window, peering out at the quiet street. The sight of a neighbor's car disappearing into the night made her heart ache with uncertainty. I should have seen it coming, she thought, remorse tinging her voice as she whispered to herself. Had I ignored the signs for too long?

She had always believed that keeping the family together was paramount. But now, as she faced the possibility that Julia had left because things were far worse than she had let on, a new emotion stirred within her—a genuine concern for her daughter's well-being. Anne's mind raced with what-ifs. *Was Julia truly safe? Is Sarah safe?* The questions tormented her in the stillness of the night.

Setting her teacup down, Anne reached for the telephone once more. Her fingers trembled as they hovered over the dial, torn between the instinct to call Julia and the dread of hearing news that might confirm her worst fears. With a heavy sigh, she set the receiver back in its cradle. Instead, she resolved to quietly gather what information she could. Perhaps a visit to a neighbor, or a discreet inquiry at the local grocery store, would shed some light on her daughter's whereabouts.

Anne knew that Julia's departure was not merely an act of defiance—it was a cry for help, a desperate escape from a reality that had been far darker than she had ever suspected. A cold shiver ran down her spine as she acknowledged the possibility: maybe things had been worse between Julia and Ed than she had known.

Julia's gone, she whispered into the silence, her voice laced with worry rather than judgment. And as darkness settled outside, Anne sat alone with her conflicted thoughts—haunted by regret, fueled by concern, and determined that if given a chance, she would do everything in her power to help her daughter find safety and healing, even if it meant confronting truths she had long avoided.

**

Chapter 5

A New Dawn

The morning light crept through the thin curtains of the trailer, casting a warm, golden glow on the walls. Julia stirred, momentarily disoriented before remembering—she was here, in Kentucky, far from Ed. A quiet breath of relief escaped her lips.

Beside her, Sarah was still curled up in a tangle of blankets, her small fingers clutching her beloved ragged bunny. Julia smoothed her daughter's hair gently, feeling a deep sense of gratitude that they had made it here safely. Today was a new day, the first of many in their fresh start.

She slid out of bed and stretched, the mobile home was small but cozy, and most importantly, it was theirs—a safe place where Sarah could play and laugh without fear.

After a simple breakfast, Julia dropped Sarah off at the sitter's—a kind woman named Teresa who lived just a few lots over and had a small in-home daycare. It gave Julia peace of mind to know Sarah was in a safe place while she worked.

Her first day as an assistant administrative worker at the community center started smoothly. It wasn't her dream job, but it was steady, and that's what mattered right now. As she sorted through paperwork and familiarized herself with the office, she reminded herself that this was just a stepping stone.

At lunch, Julia sat alone in the small break room, stirring her tea absentmindedly. She traced the edge of the tiny box in her pocket—the mustard seed Charles had given her. His words echoed in her mind: *A little faith can grow into something strong.* She smiled softly, feeling the strength in that sentiment.

By the time she finished her shift and returned home, exhaustion tugged at her, but it was a different kind of exhaustion—one born from progress, not fear. She picked up Sarah from Teresa's and carried her inside, the little girl sleepy but content.

That evening, as Julia made Sarah's small bed with the few linens she had, she listened to the quietness of the mobile home park settling in for the night. Outside, a single lamp near the front steps cast a warm glow, welcoming them into this new chapter.

Julia tucked Sarah in, watching as her daughter hugged her bunny close and drifted to sleep. She sat on the edge of the bed for a moment, taking it all in. They had made it. They were safe.

Slipping outside, she stood on the small porch, inhaling the crisp night air. She reached into her pocket, feeling the tiny mustard seed between her fingers. It wasn't just a symbol—it was a promise.

A promise to herself. A promise to Sarah.

They were going to be okay.

**

Laying Foundations

The days began to settle into a rhythm. Mornings were a blur of getting Sarah ready, packing lunches, and rushing to drop her off at Teresa's before heading to work. Evenings were quieter—dinners at their small kitchen table, bedtime stories, and the occasional sketching session when Sarah was asleep.

Julia found a certain comfort in the predictability of it all. It wasn't perfect, but it was safe.

At work, she was catching on quickly. The administrative office at the community center was small, but the people were kind. Her supervisor, Linda, was a no-nonsense woman in her fifties who appreciated efficiency but had a soft spot for single mothers trying to make ends meet.

One afternoon, as Julia organized a filing cabinet, Linda glanced over. "You're picking things up fast," she said.

Julia smiled. "I just like to stay busy."

Linda studied her for a moment. "What did you do before this?"

"I worked at a diner," Julia admitted. "Mostly waiting tables. But I've always drawn. I used to sketch when I had time."

Linda's expression turned thoughtful. "You know, we have an art class here for kids and beginners. The instructor is retiring soon. You might want to think about it."

Julia blinked in surprise. "Me? Teach an art class?"

"Why not? You've got the skill, and you might enjoy it." Linda shrugged before turning back to her computer, leaving Julia with a swirl of new possibilities in her mind.

That evening, after picking up Sarah and making dinner, Julia found herself at the small kitchen table, sketchbook in hand. She hadn't drawn in days, too caught up in adjusting to her new life. Now, with a deep breath, she let the pencil glide across the page.

A face took shape—gentle eyes, kind smile. Charles.

She hesitated, her fingers pausing over the lines she had just drawn. She hadn't reached out to him since leaving. He had given her space, and she appreciated that. But now, for the first time, she found herself missing their conversations, the quiet understanding he had always offered.

Maybe it was time to call.

Julia closed the sketchbook, running her fingers over its worn cover. Tomorrow. She would think about it tomorrow.

For now, she had a daughter to tuck into bed and a future to keep building, one steady step at a time.

**

Chapter 6

Reaching Out

The next evening, after dinner and Sarah's bedtime routine, Julia sat on the couch, phone in hand, staring at the screen. It had been weeks since she last spoke to Charles. He had given her space, and she had been grateful for it, but now… she missed their talks. She missed his steady presence.

Taking a deep breath, she scrolled through her contacts until she found his name. Her fingers hovered over the call button. What if he had moved on? What if he had decided she was better off without any reminders of the life she left behind?

Before she could second-guess herself, she tapped the screen.

The phone rang once. Twice. Then—

"Julia?"

His voice was warm, familiar, and instantly grounding.

"Hey, Charles." She smiled, leaning back into the couch. "I—uh—I just wanted to call. See how you're doing."

A pause. Then a soft chuckle. "I was wondering when I'd hear from you."

Her heart skipped slightly. "You were?"

"Yeah." His voice was gentle. "I figured you needed time to settle in. How's everything going?"

Julia exhaled. "It's… different. But good. Sarah's adjusting, and I found a job at a community center. It's not the diner, but it's steady."

"That's great, Julia. I knew you'd land on your feet."

She hesitated, then admitted, "I still think about everything. About the diner. About you."

Another pause. "I think about you too," he said, quieter this time.

Something warm settled in her chest. For the first time since leaving, she didn't feel like she was just surviving—she felt like she was beginning to live.

They talked for nearly an hour, catching up on the little things. He told her how the diner wasn't the same without her, how Ed had come storming in once looking for her, but Charles hadn't given him anything. She was safe.

By the time they hung up, Julia felt lighter. Stronger.

Maybe the past wasn't something to run from forever. Maybe, just maybe, some pieces of it were worth holding onto.

**

Lingering Thoughts

As the days passed, Julia found herself thinking about Charles more and more. It wasn't intentional, at least not at first. His voice still echoed in her mind from their phone call, the warmth in his tone, the way he had said her name. It had been weeks since she left her old life behind, yet Charles remained in her thoughts like an unfinished sketch—lines drawn but not yet fully shaded in.

At work, while organizing files or answering phones, her mind would wander. What was he doing right now? Was he at the diner, sketching between customers? Did he think about her as much as she thought about him?

At night, after Sarah was asleep, she would sit on the small porch of the trailer, the cool Kentucky breeze brushing against her skin, and wonder if she had left behind more than just a painful past. Had she also left behind something—someone—who had been quietly becoming important to her?

She wasn't ready for anything more than friendship, not yet. But the idea of Charles, of what they could be someday, lingered in the corners of her mind like the gentle strokes of a paintbrush on a blank canvas.

One evening, as she tucked Sarah in, her daughter looked up at her sleepily and murmured, "Mama, do you miss our old home?"

Julia hesitated, brushing a strand of hair from Sarah's forehead. "I miss some things," she admitted softly.

"Like what?"

She smiled faintly. "Like a good friend."

Sarah's eyes drooped closed, satisfied with the answer, but Julia stayed there for a moment longer, her heart caught in a quiet, unspoken truth.

She missed Charles. More than she was willing to admit.

**

Bridging the Distance

At first, Julia hesitated to call Charles too often. She told herself she didn't want to be a burden, that he had his own life back in Ohio. But the more she tried to push the thought of him aside, the more she found herself reaching for her phone.

The second call came a few days after their first. It was late, Sarah had been tucked in for the night, and Julia sat on the small couch with a warm cup of tea in her hands. The loneliness of starting over was heavier than she'd expected, and before she could talk herself out of it, she dialed his number.

"Julia?" His voice was surprised but pleased, and just hearing it made her relax.

"Hey," she said, feeling a little shy. "I just—uh, I hope I'm not calling too late."

"No, not at all," he assured her. "I was just finishing up some sketches. How are you?"

And just like that, they talked for nearly an hour. She told him about her new job, about how Sarah was adjusting, and even about the little quirks of living in the trailer park—like how her neighbor, an older woman named Mrs. Murphy insisted on bringing her baked goods every other day. Charles listened intently, asking questions, laughing in all the right places. When she turned the conversation to him, he told her about work, about the diner, about how things were mostly the same but a little quieter without her there.

"You're missed, you know," he admitted, his voice softer than before.

Something in her chest tightened. "I miss you too," she found herself saying, her voice barely above a whisper.

After that, the calls became more frequent. Sometimes it was just a quick check-in, other times they'd stay on the phone for hours, talking about everything and nothing. Julia found herself looking forward to them, the way she could be completely herself with him, no pretenses, no fear.

One evening, after a particularly long day at work, she called him just to hear his voice.

"You're calling me a lot these days," Charles teased gently.

"Am I?" she replied with a smile he couldn't see.

"I'm not complaining," he said. "I like it."

Julia bit her lip, warmth spreading through her. She hadn't expected this connection to grow so naturally, but with Charles, everything felt easy. Safe.

Maybe, just maybe, she was finally learning what it felt like to truly be free.

**

Chapter 7

A Desperate Plea

Ed sat in his car outside Anne's house, gripping the steering wheel so tightly his knuckles turned white. He had spent the last few weeks consumed by anger, but that fire had burned itself down into something else—something raw and hollow. Regret.

He never thought Julia would actually leave. She had threatened before, sure, but she had always stayed. Always forgiven him. But this time was different. She was gone, and she had taken Sarah with her.

Taking a deep breath, he stepped out of the car and walked up the familiar front porch. The house still smelled like coffee and cinnamon, just as it always had. His stomach twisted as he knocked.

Anne answered the door, her expression cautious. "Ed."

"Anne," he said, his voice stiff with emotion. "Can I come in?"

She hesitated but finally stepped aside, letting him in. He had been here countless times before, but today, the house felt different—colder.

They sat in the living room, an awkward silence stretching between them before Ed finally spoke.

"I know you don't want to see me," he admitted, his voice quieter than usual. "But I—I need to say something."

Anne folded her arms. "Go on."

He swallowed hard. "I was wrong. About everything. I know that now." He rubbed his face with his hands, struggling to find the words. "I took Julia for granted. I let my temper get the best of me, and I—" His voice cracked, and he exhaled sharply. "I drove her away."

Anne's lips pressed into a thin line. "You didn't just 'drive her away from you, Ed. You pushed her away from me too."

The truth of her words hit him like a slap, but he didn't argue. "I know," he admitted. "I know I messed up. And I know I don't deserve her back. But if you talk to her… if she ever calls… could you just tell her that I realize it now? That I'm willing to change."

Anne sighed, studying him carefully. "Ed, I've known you for a long time. And I don't doubt that you have regrets. But change?" She shook her head. "That's not something you can promise overnight."

"I mean it," he insisted. "I—I'd do anything to fix this."

Anne sighed again, softer this time. "I'll tell her, if she calls me. But whether she believes you, or wants anything to do with you, that's her choice."

Ed nodded, accepting what little hope he could get. He stood to leave, glancing around the house one last time, feeling like a stranger in a place that used to feel like home.

As he walked back to his car, he realized something painful but true—words alone wouldn't be enough. If he ever wanted a chance at redemption, he would have to prove it.

**

A Plan to Prove It

Ed sat in his car outside Anne's house for a long time after their conversation, his mind racing. The old anger still simmered beneath his skin, but it was no longer directed at Julia. It was at himself.

She was gone. She had taken Sarah and left, and for the first time, he truly understood why. But understanding didn't make it easier to accept. He had lost control of everything, and he hated that feeling more than anything.

His hands tightened on the steering wheel. How could he prove he was willing to change when he didn't even know where she was? He had no way to contact her, no way to show her he could be different. The thought sent a wave of frustration crashing over him.

Then another thought crept in—he didn't need to find her right away. He needed to become the kind of man she might one day be willing to speak to again.

Ed had never been good at self-reflection, but now, as he stared at his own weary, unshaven face in the rearview mirror, he saw someone he barely recognized.

"I need to fix myself first," he muttered. It was a foreign idea to him—change. Not just words, not just empty apologies, but actual, lasting change. He had always thought of himself as the one in control, the one who made the rules. But now? Now, he was just a man who had pushed away the only people who ever really mattered.

But where did he even begin?

His first instinct was to track her down. To call in favors, to search, to demand answers. But he forced himself to take a breath. That wasn't what she needed from him. If he hunted her down now, he'd only be proving her right—that he was someone she needed to run from.

No, if there was any chance of seeing Sarah again, of having a relationship with his daughter, he needed to take a different path. He needed to prove—to himself as much as to Julia—that he could be better.

His jaw tightened with determination.

Step one: Get his temper under control.

Step two: Get his life in order.

Step three: Wait.

If Julia ever reached out, if she ever wanted to talk, he had to be someone worth talking to. And until then, he had to live with the consequences of what he had done.

With a deep sigh, Ed put his car in gear and pulled away from Anne's house. For the first time in years, he felt like he had no control over what came next.

And that terrified him.

**

Chapter 8

A Neighborly Connection

A few weeks into her new routine, Julia found herself crossing paths more often with Mrs. Murphy, the elderly woman who lived in the mobile home next door. She was a petite woman with soft gray curls and kind eyes that always seemed to notice more than she let on.

One evening, as Julia carried a small bag of groceries from the car, she heard the familiar creak of Mrs. Murphy's screen door.

"Julia, dear, you look like you could use a little rest," Mrs. Murphy called from her porch, as she took a seat in her well-worn rocking chair.

Julia smiled, pausing to adjust the weight of the bag. "Long day at work, but I'm getting used to it."

Mrs. Murphy nodded knowingly. "New beginnings take time to settle into. Come sit for a moment—if Sarah's all squared away, of course."

Julia hesitated, then gave a small laugh. "She's inside finishing up her coloring. I think I have a few minutes." She stepped onto the porch, sinking into the cushioned chair beside her neighbor.

The evening air was cool, and the sound of crickets filled the quiet spaces between them. Mrs. Murphy didn't pry, but her presence alone felt like an open invitation.

After a moment, Julia exhaled. "I left my husband," she admitted softly, watching the shadows stretch along the ground.

Mrs. Murphy's rocking slowed just a little. "I wondered," she said gently. "Didn't want to assume, but I could tell there was more to your move than just a fresh start."

Julia swallowed the lump in her throat. "I had to go. For me and for Sarah."

Mrs. Murphy reached over, giving her hand a comforting pat. "Then you did the right thing."

Julia blinked back the sudden sting in her eyes. "It's just...hard. I keep expecting him to show up. And part of me wonders if I should have tried harder. But I couldn't stay—not with how things were."

Mrs. Murphy squeezed her hand. "Sweetheart, trying harder doesn't change people who don't want to change. You did what you had to do. And you're not alone here."

Julia smiled, warmth filling her chest. She hadn't realized how much she needed to hear that.

For the first time since arriving, she felt just a little more at home.

**

Neighborly

The porch was quiet except for the rhythmic creaking of Mrs. Murphy's rocker and the distant hum of a television from another trailer. Julia hesitated, staring at her hands as she paused.

Mrs. Murphy didn't rush her, just waited, her presence warm and patient.

Finally, Julia sighed and continued, choosing her words carefully. “Ed wasn’t always like this. When we first got together, he was… different. He was kind, thoughtful, and we had fun together. He used to leave me little notes, bring home flowers for no reason. He was the kind of guy I thought I could spend my life with.”

Mrs. Murphy gave a small nod. “Love can start that way—full of promise.”

Julia’s lips pressed together. “But somewhere along the way, things changed. Maybe I just didn’t see the signs at first, or maybe I ignored them because I didn’t want to believe it. It started small—little criticisms, like the way I dressed or the way I cooked. Then it was my job at the diner. He didn’t like me working, but we needed the money. He’d tell me I should be home with Sarah, that no wife of his should have to work. But it never came from a place of concern—it was about control.”

Mrs. Murphy let out a quiet sigh, rocking gently. “And then?”

Julia swallowed hard. “Then it got worse. He started yelling more, throwing things. One time he punched a hole in the wall right next to my head. I told myself he was just stressed, that he’d never actually hurt me.”

She looked down at the porch floor, shaking her head. “But I was wrong. The first time he hit me, I stood there in shock. I couldn’t believe it. He apologized after—said he lost his temper, that he didn’t mean it. He swore it wouldn’t happen again.”

Mrs. Murphy’s eyes darkened with sadness, her hands gripping the arms of her chair. “But it did.”

Julia nodded. "Yeah. And after a while, the apologies stopped. He'd act like it never happened, like I was the one overreacting and the worst part was, she let out a shaky breath. I started to believe him."

Mrs. Murphy reached over, resting a gentle hand over Julia's. "Oh, sweetheart."

Julia fought the tears burning behind her eyes. "I thought if I just did everything right, if I could keep him from getting mad, then maybe things would go back to the way they used to be. But no matter what I did, it was never enough."

Mrs. Murphy's grip tightened. "Abusers don't need a reason, Julia. They just need control."

Julia looked down at her lap. "I was scared. Not just for me, but for Sarah. I didn't want her to grow up thinking that's what love looks like. I didn't want her to see her mother afraid all the time."

She finally lifted her eyes, finding comfort in Mrs. Murphy's understanding gaze. "That's why I left. I had to."

Mrs. Murphy nodded, her voice firm but kind. "You did the bravest thing a mother can do. You protected your child. And yourself."

A tear slipped down Julia's cheek, but this time, she didn't wipe it away. Instead, she let out a breath she felt like she'd been holding for years.

For the first time in a long time, she felt understood.

Julia let out a small breath, as if releasing some of the weight she had been carrying. She glanced toward the darkening sky and then back at Mrs. Murphy with a grateful smile.

"Thank you for listening," she said softly. "I don't really talk about all of this much, but… it helps. It really does."

Mrs. Murphy reached out and gave Julia's hand a gentle squeeze. "Anytime, dear. You don't have to carry it all alone. And you don't have to rush through healing, either."

Julia nodded, blinking away the moisture in her eyes. "I should get back to Sarah now. She's probably wondering where I am."

Mrs. Murphy gave an understanding smile. "Of course. That little girl is lucky to have you, Julia. And if you ever need anything, even just a cup of tea and a quiet place to sit, my door is always open."

Julia felt warmth spread through her chest at the kindness. "That means a lot. Really."

She stood up and tucked her jacket around her, the cool evening breeze settling in as she walked back toward her trailer, she felt a little lighter. The past still lingered, but for the first time in a long time, she felt like she wasn't carrying it alone.

**

The Visit

Over the next several weeks, Julia and Charles spoke more frequently. Their conversations, once casual check-ins, had grown longer, filled with laughter and shared stories. Julia found herself looking forward to their calls, her heart lifting whenever she saw his name appear on her phone.

One evening, as she sat on the small couch with Sarah asleep in the other room, her phone buzzed. It was Charles.

"Hey, you," she answered, a smile already forming.

"Hey yourself," he replied, his voice warm. "How was your day?"

They talked for a while about work, Sarah, and even Mrs. Murphy. But after a pause, Charles's tone shifted slightly, becoming more serious.

"Julia, I've been thinking... I want to come see you."

Her breath caught for a second. "Come here?"

"Yeah," he said softly. "I know you've been through a lot, and I don't want to push. But I'd really like to see you. No pressure—just a visit. What do you think?"

Julia hesitated, her mind a whirlwind of thoughts. She wanted to see him—there was no denying that. But was she ready? Would it complicate things? Still, the idea of having Charles there, even for a short time, filled her with warmth.

"I... I think I'd like that," she finally admitted.

His relieved chuckle made her heart skip. "Good. Then I'll start figuring out when I can come."

Julia leaned back against the couch, the warmth of the moment settling over her. For the first time in a long time, she felt something unfamiliar but welcome—hope.

The next evening, after dinner, Julia sat on the couch with Sarah, who was curled up beside her, brushing her doll's hair. Julia had spent the entire day thinking about how to bring up the subject of Charles' visit, wanting to approach it in a way that wouldn't confuse or upset her daughter.

Taking a breath, she gently smoothed Sarah's hair. "Sweetheart, I want to talk to you about something."

Sarah looked up from her doll, her bright eyes curious. "What is it, Mommy?"

Julia hesitated for a moment, then smiled. "Remember my friend Charles? The one I talk to on the phone sometimes?"

Sarah nodded slowly. "Yeah… the one from back home?"

"That's right," Julia said. "Well, he's going to come visit us in a few days."

Sarah blinked, tilting her head. "Here? At our house?"

"Yes, just for a little while," Julia assured her. "I wanted to tell you because I always want you to know what's going on."

Sarah played with the hem of her shirt, thinking. "Is he nice?"

Julia smiled warmly. "He's very nice, sweetheart. He's kind, like Uncle Rick, and he cares about us."

Sarah was quiet for a moment, her little fingers still fidgeting. Then, she looked up at Julia with uncertainty. "What about Daddy?"

Julia felt her heart squeeze at the question, though she'd known it was coming. Keeping her voice gentle, she tucked a stray curl behind Sarah's ear. "What about him, sweetheart?"

Sarah's voice was barely above a whisper. "Is he coming too?"

Julia shook her head softly. "No, honey. Daddy isn't coming. This is just Charles visiting us."

Sarah chewed her lip, then asked, "Does he know Daddy?"

"No, he doesn't."

Sarah seemed to think that over, still gripping her doll. "Does he know me?"

Julia smiled gently. "Kind of, I've told him all about you." And he met you at the diner the day we left.

Sarah finally looked up, searching Julia's face. "Will he like me?"

"Oh, baby," Julia said, pulling Sarah into a hug. "Of course he will. You're the sweetest, most wonderful little girl. Charles is just a friend, and you don't have to be nervous, okay?"

Sarah rested her head against Julia's chest. "Okay," she murmured. Then, after a pause, she added, "Maybe he can play dolls with me."

Julia chuckled softly. "Maybe. We'll see."

Sarah seemed satisfied with that answer, and Julia kissed the top of her head, holding her a little tighter.

The visit would bring change, whether small or big, and Julia wasn't sure how it would unfold. But for now, knowing that Sarah was open to it, even in her small way, made her feel just a little more at peace.

**

Chapter 9

Charles sat at his small kitchen table, his laptop open in front of him. The soft glow of the screen reflected in his eyes as he scrolled through search results, familiarizing himself with the area Julia now called home. He had been looking forward to this visit since the moment she agreed, and now that the trip was set in motion, he wanted to make it special.

His fingers tapped against the side of his coffee mug as he thought. He didn't want to overwhelm her—this visit wasn't about grand gestures or anything too serious. But he did want to give her something she hadn't had in a long time: a simple, peaceful evening out, free from worry.

Clicking through a few local websites, he found a small, family-owned restaurant that looked promising. It had a cozy, relaxed atmosphere, perfect for conversation. Not too fancy, but nicer than the average diner. He smiled, bookmarking the page.

Next, he looked into places they might go afterward. There was a little park by a lake not too far from where she lived, and from the photos, it looked like a beautiful place to walk and talk. He imagined them strolling along the water's edge, maybe sharing stories about their pasts, and their dreams for the future.

His phone buzzed beside him, and for a moment, he wondered if it was Julia. But when he saw it was just a work email, he sighed and set the phone back down.

He had no illusions about this trip—Julia had been through a lot, and she was still finding her footing. But something deep inside him told him that this visit was important, not just for her but for him as well. He had grown fond of her, more than he ever expected, and he wanted to show her that she had someone in her corner, someone who genuinely cared.

Leaning back in his chair, he closed his laptop with a sense of quiet determination. In just a few days, he'd be there. And whether it was just a friendly dinner or the start of something more, he was ready to show Julia that she deserved kindness, laughter, and a fresh start.

Charles reopened his laptop, rubbing the back of his neck as he considered the long drive ahead. It wasn't an impossible trip to make in one day, but if the evening went well, he didn't want to rush out just to make it back home that night. He figured it would be smarter to have a hotel lined up, just in case.

He clicked through a few options, looking for something clean and comfortable but not too extravagant. He wasn't trying to impress Julia with luxury—just being there for her was enough. Finally, he settled on a modest but well-rated hotel about ten minutes from her place. It had good reviews, and that was all he really needed. He booked a room for one night, knowing he could extend it if necessary.

As he confirmed the reservation, he exhaled slowly. This was happening. He was really going to see her again, in a new place, in this new chapter of her life. He hoped she wouldn't feel nervous about his visit—he didn't want to add any pressure. He just wanted to be someone she could rely on, someone she felt safe with.

His thoughts drifted to Sarah. He knew Julia had told her about his visit, but how would the little girl react to meeting him? He didn't want to be a stranger who made her uncomfortable, so he made a mental note to take it slow, to let Sarah set the tone. He smiled, thinking back to when Julia had mentioned how much Sarah loved to color. Maybe he'd bring her a small coloring book and some crayons, something simple to break the ice.

Closing his laptop again, he sat back in his chair and stared out the window. In just a couple of days, he'd be on the road, heading toward a woman who had been on his mind more than he ever expected. He wasn't sure what this visit would mean for the two of them, but he knew one thing for certain—he wanted to be in her life, in whatever way she was ready for.

Now, all that was left to do was wait.

**

Julia's Anticipation

As the day of Charles's visit approached, Julia found herself nervously tidying the small trailer, wiping down already-clean surfaces and rearranging things that didn't really need rearranging. She kept telling herself it was just a visit from a friend, but she couldn't deny the fluttering in her chest every time she thought about seeing Charles again.

Sarah, completely oblivious to her mother's nerves, sat on the floor nearby, playing with her bunny and some crayons. "Mommy, do I get to meet your friend?" she asked, tilting her head curiously.

Julia smiled, smoothing her hands over the couch cushion. "Yes, sweet girl. You'll meet him when he gets here, but he and I are going to go out for a little bit in the evening."

Sarah frowned slightly. "Where will I go?"

"That's what I need to figure out." Julia sighed, realizing she hadn't yet arranged for a sitter. Just then, a knock on the door startled her. She opened it to find Mrs. Murphy standing on the small porch, a warm smile on her face.

"Good afternoon, dear," the elderly woman greeted, peering inside. "I was just wondering if you needed anything from the store. I'm making a run into town."

Julia hesitated for a second before an idea struck her. "Actually, Mrs. Murphy, I was wondering if you'd be up for some company tomorrow evening. I have a friend visiting, and I was hoping to find someone to stay with Sarah for a few hours."

Mrs. Murphy's eyes twinkled. "Oh, I'd love to. You know I enjoy spending time with that little girl of yours."

Sarah perked up at the conversation. "Really? You'll stay with me?"

Mrs. Murphy chuckled. "Of course, sweetheart. We can have a little movie night, maybe bake some cookies if your mom says it's okay."

Julia let out a relieved breath. "That sounds perfect. Thank you so much."

"Think nothing of it," Mrs. Murphy said with a wave of her hand. Then she gave Julia a knowing look. "Now, don't you go worrying too much, dear. It's just a visit. Enjoy yourself."

Julia nodded, but as she closed the door behind her neighbor, she realized she wasn't just worried—she was excited. It had been a long time since she felt this kind of anticipation. And though she wasn't sure what the evening with Charles would bring, she knew one thing for certain—she was looking forward to it.

**

Charles Arrives

The next day, Julia found herself checking the clock more often than she cared to admit. She had spent the morning keeping busy—taking Sarah to the park, running a few errands, and making sure the trailer was presentable. Even though she knew Charles wouldn't care about the state of her small home, she still wanted everything to feel welcoming.

By mid-afternoon, Sarah was down for a nap, and Julia finally took a moment to breathe. She stood in front of the mirror, smoothing her hair and second-guessing her outfit. It wasn't a date, she reminded herself—just a visit from a friend. A friend who made her heart race a little faster than it should.

A crunch of gravel outside made her stomach flip. Peeking out the window, she saw Charles stepping out of his car, stretching slightly from the long drive. He looked good—casual in jeans and a button-down shirt, but still effortlessly put together.

Taking a deep breath, Julia opened the door just as he reached the small porch.

"Hey," he said, flashing her that familiar warm smile. "I made it."

She smiled back, suddenly feeling lighter. "You did. Long drive?"

"Not too bad," he said, glancing around. "This place suits you."

She wasn't sure what he meant by that, but she took it as a compliment. "Come in," she said, stepping aside.

As Charles entered, he glanced around the modest space, taking in the simple but cozy touches. His eyes landed on a small sketchpad on the table. "Still drawing?"

Julia nodded, feeling slightly self-conscious. "A little. When I have time."

Before he could say more, the soft shuffle of small feet caught their attention. Sarah stood in the hallway, rubbing her sleepy eyes and clutching her bunny.

Julia smiled and knelt down. "Hey, sweetheart. This is my friend Charles. Remember I told you he was coming to visit?"

Sarah blinked at him for a moment, then nodded. "Hi," she said shyly.

Charles crouched slightly to her level and pulled something from behind his back—a small coloring book and a brand-new pack of crayons wrapped neatly with a ribbon. "I brought you a little something," he said with a warm smile. "Thought you might like it."

Sarah's eyes widened as she took the gift, flipping through the pages of the coloring book. "Wow! Thank you!"

"You're welcome," Charles said, clearly pleased by her reaction. "I heard you like to color."

She nodded enthusiastically. "I do! Mommy draws pictures too."

"She does," Charles agreed, glancing at Julia with a knowing smile. "She's pretty good, isn't she?"

Sarah beamed. "Yeah!"

Julia shook her head, touched by the thoughtful gesture. "That was really sweet of you."

Charles shrugged. "Figured I should bring something for the little lady of the house."

Sarah, now focused on picking the perfect color from the set, was already at the table, deeply engrossed in her new activity.

Charles stood and looked at Julia. "So, you ready for tonight?"

Julia took a deep breath. "Yeah, I think I am."

And for the first time in a long while, she actually meant it.

**

Mrs. Murphy's Gentle Reminder

Julia gathered Sarah's things—a small blanket, her bunny, and the new coloring book Charles had given her. Instead of having Mrs. Murphy come over, Julia decided it would be better to walk Sarah to her trailer. It felt more natural, and it gave her a few extra minutes to settle her nerves before the evening ahead.

The evening air was warm but carried a slight breeze as they made their way down the gravel path. Sarah skipped along beside her, clutching her bunny in one hand and holding Julia's fingers with the other.

"You'll have fun with Mrs. Murphy, sweetheart," Julia said as they approached the older woman's front porch. "She's got those cookies you like."

Sarah grinned. "And she lets me have two."

Julia chuckled just as Mrs. Murphy opened the door with a warm smile. "Well, well, look who's here," she said, stepping aside to let them in. "Come in, little one. I've got everything ready for you."

Sarah didn't hesitate, already making herself at home as she placed her bunny on the couch and set her coloring book on the coffee table.

Mrs. Murphy turned to Julia, taking her in with her wise, knowing eyes. "You look lovely, dear."

Julia exhaled, smoothing the front of her blouse. "Thank you."

Mrs. Murphy studied her for a moment, then reached out and gently patted Julia's arm. "Remember, it's just a visit."

Julia swallowed, nodding. "I know."

The older woman smiled knowingly. "It's okay to be nervous, but don't let it stop you from enjoying yourself."

Julia let out a small laugh. "Was it that obvious?"

Mrs. Murphy chuckled. "A little."

Julia sighed, glancing at Sarah, who was already lost in her coloring. "Thank you for watching her."

Mrs. Murphy waved a hand. "Oh, hush. You go enjoy yourself. She'll be just fine here with me."

Julia bent down to kiss Sarah's head. "Be good for Mrs. Murphy, okay?"

"I will, Mommy," Sarah said without looking up, already choosing the next color for her picture.

With one last grateful look at Mrs. Murphy, Julia turned and stepped back out into the evening air. As she walked toward Charles' car, she took a deep breath, trying to steady her nerves.

It was just a visit.

But she couldn't ignore the way her heart fluttered at the thought of what this evening might bring.

**

A Step Into Something New

Charles stood beside his car, leaning casually against the door as Julia approached. His warm smile eased some of the nervous energy swirling in her stomach.

"You look great," he said, his gaze holding a sincerity that made her cheeks warm.

"Thanks," she replied, tucking a loose strand of hair behind her ear. "You clean up nice yourself."

He chuckled and opened the car door for her. "Ready?"

She nodded, sliding into the passenger seat. As he got in on his side and started the engine, she let out a slow breath. It had been years since she'd been out with someone who wasn't Ed, and though she knew this wasn't a date, it still felt… different.

The drive was peaceful, their conversation light as Charles pointed out the scenic views along the way. The rolling hills, the golden glow of the evening sun filtering through the trees, and the occasional glimpse of a farmhouse nestled in the distance—it was the kind of beauty Julia hadn't taken the time to notice in a long while.

"This is a beautiful area," Charles said, his tone easy.

Julia nodded. "Yeah, it really is. I guess I've been so focused on everything else that I haven't taken a moment to appreciate it."

Charles glanced over at her briefly before returning his eyes to the road. "Sometimes, a change of scenery can be a fresh start in more ways than one."

She let his words settle, feeling their weight. A fresh start. That's what she had been working toward, wasn't it?

When they arrived at the restaurant, Charles parked and quickly moved to open her door before she could do it herself. She raised an eyebrow at him.

"Chivalry's not dead," he said with a grin.

She smiled, shaking her head as she stepped out.

Inside, the restaurant had a warm, cozy feel with dim lighting and soft music in the background. They were seated near a window, and Julia couldn't help but glance outside for a moment, still adjusting to the idea of being out like this, free from the weight of her old life.

As they looked over the menus, Charles leaned in slightly. "So, how's the new job treating you?"

"It's good," Julia said. "It's steady, and I like the routine. It's not my dream job, but it's a start."

"And your art?" he asked.

She hesitated, then sighed. "I haven't really had time for it lately. Between the job, settling in, and making sure Sarah is adjusting, I just…"

"Hey," he said gently, "it's okay. You've had a lot on your plate. But don't forget that part of yourself, Julia. You're an artist—that doesn't just go away."

His words struck something deep inside her, something she had been pushing aside. She nodded slowly. "You're right. I don't want to lose that part of me."

Charles smiled. "Good. Because I'd love to see what you create when you finally have the space to let it all out."

Their food arrived, and the conversation flowed easily. Julia found herself truly relaxing, enjoying the moment. She had forgotten what it felt like to have someone genuinely listen, to talk without worrying about saying the wrong thing.

When they finished eating, Charles stood and held out a hand. "I was thinking… there's a little park not far from here. I saw it online when I was looking at things to do in your area. Feel like a walk?"

Julia hesitated for only a second before nodding. "Yeah. That sounds nice."

As they strolled through the park, the night air was refreshing, carrying the scent of fresh grass.. Julia wrapped her arms around herself, not from cold, but from the unfamiliar comfort of simply *being* in the moment.

"I wasn't sure if you'd say yes to this," Charles admitted, glancing at her. "To coming out tonight."

Julia looked over at him, surprised by the vulnerability in his voice. "Why?"

He shrugged. "I know you've got a lot on your mind. And I know trusting people again… well, it's not easy."

She stopped walking for a moment, considering his words. "No, it's not," she admitted. Then, with a small smile, she added, "But you make it feel easier."

Charles met her gaze, something unspoken passing between them before he nodded. "Good. Because I'm not going anywhere, Julia. Not unless you want me to."

Her chest tightened—not in fear, but in something she wasn't quite ready to name.

They continued their walk, the night wrapping around them like a quiet promise, and the conversation coming so easy Julia couldn't believe this was all real.

**

The drive back to Julia's home was filled with an easy silence. The night had been something she hadn't expected—comfortable, reassuring, and almost *normal*. As they neared the trailer park, she found herself wishing the drive was just a little longer.

Charles pulled into the small gravel driveway, shifting the car into park but not immediately turning off the engine. The soft glow from the porch light illuminated the front steps, and Julia could see the faint silhouette of Mrs. Murphy's lace curtains shifting in her window. She was likely still awake, making sure everything was as it should be.

Julia turned toward Charles, her fingers lightly running over the hem of her sweater. "Thanks for tonight," she said, her voice softer than she intended.

He looked at her for a moment, a small smile tugging at his lips. "No, thank *you*. I enjoyed it."

She exhaled as the corners of her mouth curved upward. "It's been a long time since I've had a night like this."

Charles tilted his head slightly, studying her expression. "You deserve more of them, Julia. And I hope… I get to be a part of them."

Her chest tightened again at his words, but this time, she didn't push the feeling away. Instead, she nodded. "I'd like that."

For a brief moment, it seemed like he wanted to say something more, but instead, he reached for the door handle. "I'll walk you to the door."

"You don't have to," she started, but he was already stepping out.

She smiled to herself, before following his lead. The gravel crunched beneath their steps as they approached the porch. Julia turned toward him once they reached the door, the soft light casting warm shadows across his face.

"Well," she said, shifting slightly.

"Well," he echoed, his hands slipping into his pockets. "I guess this is good night."

She nodded, holding his gaze. "Good night, Charles."

He hesitated just a fraction of a second before giving her a small, knowing smile. "Sleep well, Julia."

She stepped inside, closing the door gently behind her. Pressing her back against it, she let out a slow breath. Through the window, she watched Charles walk back to his car, the headlights flashing on as he pulled away.

A warmth lingered in her chest, something unfamiliar but not unwelcome.

For the first time in a long time, she felt like something new was beginning.

**

A Gentle End to the Evening

Julia took a moment to steady herself before pushing off the door and heading across the small yard to Mrs. Murphy's trailer. The soft glow from inside cast warm light through the lace curtains, and she could see the faint outline of Mrs. Murphy sitting in her armchair.

She knocked lightly before opening the door, stepping inside to find Sarah curled up on the couch with her raggedy bunny, her tiny fingers still loosely holding a crayon. A mostly colored page from her new coloring book rested beside her, filled with bright, mismatched colors.

Mrs. Murphy looked up from her knitting with a knowing smile. "You're back earlier than I expected, dear."

Settling onto the edge of the couch next to Sarah, she gently ran her fingers through Sarah's hair, brushing it back as the little girl stirred.

Mrs. Murphy set her knitting aside. "And how was it?"

Julia glanced over at the older woman, hesitating just a moment before allowing herself to smile. "It was… nice."

Mrs. Murphy raised an eyebrow, clearly waiting for more.

Julia let out a breathy chuckle. "Okay, it was really nice. He took me to dinner, we had a good talk, and then we walked through this little park he found. It was peaceful… easy." She shook her head slightly. "I don't think I've had a night like that in years."

Mrs. Murphy's eyes softened. "You deserve nice things, Julia."

Julia met her gaze, feeling an unexpected lump form in her throat. She swallowed it down, nodding. "Thank you for watching Sarah."

The older woman waved a dismissive hand. "Oh, we had a grand time. She colored, we read a story, and she was out like a light before she could finish telling me about the bunnies in the park you went to."

Julia smiled, glancing down at her sleeping daughter. “She does love bunnies.”

Mrs. Murphy gave her a pointed look. “And what about *you*? Do you think you’ll see him again?”

Julia hesitated, running a gentle hand over Sarah’s back. “I think so. I *hope* so.”

Mrs. Murphy’s smile deepened. “Good. It’s about time someone reminded you what it feels like to be cared for.”

Julia exhaled, shaking her head with amusement. “Alright, before you start planning a wedding, let me get Sarah home.”

Mrs. Murphy chuckled as Julia carefully lifted Sarah into her arms, the little girl shifting slightly but not waking. As she stepped toward the door, Mrs. Murphy’s voice stopped her.

“Julia.”

She turned back.

“You’re allowed to be happy.”

Julia held her gaze for a long moment before nodding. “Goodnight, Mrs. Murphy.”

“Goodnight, dear.”

With Sarah snuggled against her, Julia stepped out into the cool night air, walking back toward their trailer. As she reached the front door, she glanced up at the sky, the stars twinkling softly above.

For the first time in a long while, she allowed herself to believe that maybe—just maybe—happiness wasn't so far out of reach.

**

Chapter 10

Calling Anne

The days turned into weeks, and for the first time in what felt like forever, Julia's life began to feel *hers*. The weight of constant worry was lifting, replaced by a steady rhythm of work, home, and quiet evenings with Sarah.

Her job at the office had turned out to be a good fit. The work was predictable, and the pay was steady—enough to cover rent, groceries, and a little extra to tuck away for emergencies. For the first time in years, she wasn't watching every dollar in fear that Ed might waste it on a whim or leave her scrambling to make ends meet.

Sarah had adjusted well, too. The babysitter Julia had found—a kind woman named Teresa, who watched a few other children from her home—had been a blessing. Sarah seemed to enjoy being around the other kids, and Julia felt at ease knowing her daughter was safe and well cared for while she worked.

Even their home, as modest as it was, had started to feel like *home*. The small mobile home Rick had provided was cozy, and over time, Julia had added little touches that made it feel warm and inviting. A few of Sarah's drawings hung on the fridge, brightening the space. Julia had even found time to pick up her sketchpad again, allowing herself moments of quiet creativity after Sarah had gone to bed.

Most importantly, she no longer lived in fear.

She no longer flinched at the sound of a car pulling up, no longer braced herself when the front door opened. The anxiety that had once ruled her every move was slowly fading, replaced by something unfamiliar—*peace.*

And then, there was Charles.

Since his visit, they had fallen into a natural routine of phone calls and messages. Sometimes, it was just a quick check-in—How was your day? How's Sarah? Other times, their conversations stretched late into the evening, filled with laughter, stories, and moments that made Julia's heart feel lighter than it had in a long time.

She wasn't sure what it all meant, or where it was leading, but for now, she let herself enjoy it.

Because for the first time in years, she felt like she was *living*, not just surviving.

Julia sat on the couch, phone in hand, staring at the screen for a long moment before finally pressing the call button.

It rang twice before her mother answered. "Julia! Sweetheart, it's so good to hear from you. I was beginning to worry. I haven't heard from you since you left, and I didn't know if I should call or give you space."

Julia swallowed, guilt pressing against her chest. "I'm sorry, Mom. I didn't mean to make you worry. I just… needed time."

"I understand," Anne said, though there was an unmistakable tremor in her voice. "But I've been so worried about you and Sarah. Are you okay? Really okay?"

“We’re good, Mom,” Julia reassured her, her voice steady even as her hands trembled. “Settling in, getting used to things.”

“Oh, I’m so glad to hear that. I’ve been thinking about you constantly.” Anne’s voice was warm but tinged with something unspoken—concern, hesitation, maybe even regret. “You really left, Julia. You really left Ed. I still can’t believe it.”

Julia took a deep breath. “Mom… there’s something I need to tell you. The real reason I left.”

There was a pause on the other end. “Okay,” Anne said carefully.

Julia clenched the phone tighter. “It wasn’t just that we weren’t happy. Ed… he hurt me, Mom. He was abusive. He controlled me, he… he hit me. More times than I can count.” Her voice broke. “I didn’t want Sarah to grow up seeing that, thinking that was normal.”

Silence.

Then, a soft, trembling sound came through the line—her mother’s quiet sobs.

“Oh, Julia…” Anne whispered. “Oh, my God. I had no idea. I thought… I thought you were just having normal marriage struggles. I never imagined…” She broke off, sniffling. “How could I not see it? How could I not have known?”

“It’s not your fault, Mom,” Julia said, though her own tears threatened to fall. “I didn’t tell you. I was scared. I thought I had to make it work, no matter what. And I knew… I knew you liked Ed. I thought you’d tell me to stay.”

Anne let out a choked breath. “I might have. I hate to admit it, but I might have. And I would’ve been wrong. Julia, I am so, so sorry. My God, my baby girl, going through that alone…”

Julia swallowed the lump in her throat. "I got out. I'm safe, and Sarah is safe. That's what matters now."

Anne inhaled sharply, as if trying to pull herself together. "You're right. That is what matters. But, Julia, if I had just—if I had listened better, paid more attention—"

"Mom, please. I don't want you to blame yourself."

"But I do," Anne admitted. "I feel like I failed you. A mother is supposed to protect her daughter, and I didn't."

Julia sighed softly. "You didn't know. And I'm telling you now because… I need you to know. I need to move forward, and I need you with me."

"I'm with you," Anne said instantly, her voice thick with emotion. "From now on, I'm with you. Always."

A tear slid down Julia's cheek, but this time, it wasn't from pain—it was from relief.

"Thank you, Mom."

Anne sniffled, trying to compose herself, then cleared her throat. "And Sarah? How is she handling everything? I can't imagine how confusing this must be for her."

Julia let out a soft sigh, glancing toward Sarah's bedroom door, where she could hear the quiet hum of her daughter talking to her stuffed bunny. "She's adjusting. She asks about Ed sometimes, but I just tell her that we're in a new place now, making a new life. She doesn't seem scared, which is what I was most worried about."

Anne's voice softened. "Has she asked to see him?"

Julia hesitated. "Not really. She asks where he is, and I keep it simple. I don't want to lie to her, but I also don't want to tell her the truth in a way that makes her feel guilty or confused."

Anne sighed. "That's got to be hard. But you're doing the right thing, Julia. She's so young… she just needs love and stability right now."

"She's got that, Mom," Julia assured her. "Between me, her new routine, and even our neighbor Mrs. Murphy, she's surrounded by kindness. And she's happy."

Anne was silent for a moment, then she said, "I'd love to come visit soon. Maybe spend some time with Sarah, with you. Would that be okay?"

Julia's throat tightened. The thought of her mother visiting was both comforting and overwhelming. But Anne's tone held no judgment, no hesitation—just the genuine desire to reconnect.

"I think I'd like that," Julia admitted. "I think Sarah would, too."

Anne let out a relieved breath. "Good. Because I miss you both so much. And I want to be the mother and grandmother you both deserve."

Julia smiled, wiping at a stray tear. "That means a lot, Mom."

"Just let me know when," Anne said. "And Julia?"

"Yeah?"

“I’m proud of you. For leaving. For protecting Sarah. For standing up for yourself. It takes so much strength to do what you did.”

Julia closed her eyes, letting those words settle deep into her heart. “Thank you, Mom. That means everything.”

The call ended on a warm, promising note. For the first time in a long time, Julia truly felt like she had her mother’s support. And that, more than anything, made her feel stronger.

**

Anne had barely set the phone down, still emotionally drained from her conversation with Julia, when a sharp knock at the door made her jolt. She had a sinking feeling before she even opened it.

Standing on her porch was Ed.

His face was drawn, dark circles under his eyes, his usual smug confidence replaced by something more desperate. Anne stiffened, gripping the doorknob tightly.

"Ed," she said flatly.

"Anne, please," he exhaled, shifting his weight anxiously. "I just need to know where she is. I know you’ve talked to her. Just tell me if she’s safe. If Sarah’s safe."

Anne narrowed her eyes. "She is safe. And that's all you need to know."

Ed dragged a hand down his face, frustration clear in his stance. "Look, I know I screwed up. I know I pushed her away, but I didn't think she'd actually leave. She didn't even give me a chance to fix things!"

Anne's expression hardened. "You had plenty of chances, Ed. Don't stand there and act like this was sudden. I should've seen the signs earlier. I should've done more to help her."

He scoffed, shaking his head. "Help her? By encouraging her to take my daughter away from me?"

Anne's patience snapped. "You took her away, Ed! With every cruel word, every slap, every time you made her feel small! Do you have any idea what you've done to her?"

Ed flinched at her words, but quickly masked it with indignation. "I never meant to hurt her like that. I just—I lost my temper sometimes. Things got heated, but that doesn't mean I don't love her!"

Anne let out a slow, controlled breath, her voice quieter but firm. "Love isn't supposed to hurt like that. And Julia deserves better than what you gave her."

He stared at her, jaw tight, breathing heavily. "So that's it? You're just gonna stand by while she keeps my daughter from me?"

"Sarah isn't a possession, Ed," Anne said coldly. "She's Julia's daughter too, and Julia is doing what she feels is best for her child. You need to let them go."

His hands clenched into fists at his sides, not in aggression but in restraint. "I just… I need to see my little girl."

Anne shook her head. "That's not up to me. If Julia wants to reach out, she will. But I won't betray her trust."

For a moment, Ed looked completely lost. His shoulders sagged, his eyes darting away as if trying to process everything. Then, without another word, he turned and stalked back to his car, slamming the door shut.

Anne watched him drive away, an uneasy feeling in her gut. He wasn't going to stop looking. And that worried her more than anything.

**

Chapter 11

Starting the Divorce

A week after her emotional conversation with her mother, Julia sat in a quiet law office, her hands clasped together on the polished wooden desk in front of her. The attorney, a middle-aged woman named Glenda Calloway, flipped through a legal pad, scanning over the notes she had taken from Julia's initial explanation.

"So,"Glenda said, looking up with a calm but firm expression, "you're ready to move forward with filing for divorce?"

Julia swallowed and nodded. "Yes. I have to."

Glenda set her pen down and folded her hands. "I want to be upfront with you about what this process might look like. Since you left the state with Sarah, Ed could try to claim parental abandonment, but given the circumstances, I doubt it would hold much weight—especially if we can prove a history of abuse."

Julia tensed at the word. She knew it was the truth, but hearing it spoken so plainly made it feel heavier. "I don't have police reports," she admitted. "No official documentation. Just… my word. And maybe some witnesses who knew what was going on."

Glenda gave a small nod. "That's common in cases like yours. But don't worry. Your testimony, along with any character witnesses, can still be powerful. Plus, the fact that he hasn't officially reported Sarah missing shows that he knows he doesn't have a strong case for custody."

Julia's heart pounded at the thought of custody battles. "I don't want him to take her from me."

Glenda's voice softened. "And we'll fight to make sure that doesn't happen."

Taking a deep breath, Julia nodded again. "Okay. What's the next step?"

"We'll start by officially filing for divorce on the grounds of domestic abuse and irreconcilable differences," Glenda explained. "Then we'll serve Ed the divorce papers. He'll have a window of time to respond, and depending on how he reacts, we'll know what kind of fight we're in for."

Julia clenched her fingers together. "He's not just going to let me go," she murmured.

Glenda's gaze was steady. "Then we'll make sure he has no choice."

At that time, Julia felt like she had a real ally in this fight.

**

Chapter 12

Ed's Served

Ed sat in his dimly lit living room, a half-empty beer bottle on the coffee table in front of him. The house was too quiet, too empty. Julia's absence was something he had fought against, denying it, blaming her, trying to convince himself she'd come back. But as the days passed, and the silence stretched on, reality sank in deeper.

She was really gone.

And it was his fault.

The knock on the door startled him. He dragged himself up from the couch, running a hand through his unkempt hair as he opened it. A man in a suit stood there, holding a thick envelope.

"Edgar Thompson?" the man asked.

"Yeah," Ed replied cautiously.

The man handed over the envelope. "You've been served."

Ed stared at it for a long moment, the weight of the papers in his hand feeling heavier than it should have. He didn't even ask questions before shutting the door, his stomach twisting as he walked back inside.

He sank onto the couch and tore open the envelope, scanning the legal jargon. **Dissolution of marriage. Irreconcilable differences. Domestic abuse.**

There it was, in black and white. Julia wasn't just gone—she was making it official.

Ed exhaled sharply and rubbed his face with his hands. He couldn't deny what he'd done. The shouting, the insults, the moments of rage that had turned into bruises. He had never wanted to see himself as that kind of man, but he had become him. And now, he was paying the price.

But Sarah—he wasn't ready to give up on his daughter.

His eyes moved down the page, scanning for any mention of custody. Julia wanted full custody. He had expected that. But there was still room to negotiate visitation rights.

Setting the papers aside, Ed reached for his phone, hesitating before dialing Anne's number. He knew Julia wouldn't answer if he called her directly—if he even had her number anymore. But maybe, just maybe, Anne would listen.

After a few rings, she picked up. "Ed," she said, her voice weary.

"I got the papers," he said flatly.

There was silence on the other end, then a cautious, "I see."

Ed cleared his throat. "I know I messed up. I know why she left. But I still want to see Sarah."

Anne hesitated, and for a moment, he thought she might refuse. Then, finally, she said, "I'll talk to Julia."

Ed let out a slow breath. "Thank you."

It wasn't much, but it was something.

Ed ended the call and leaned back against the couch, staring up at the ceiling. His gut twisted as he replayed the conversation with Anne. She hadn't shut him down immediately, but there was no telling what Julia would say.

Would she let him see Sarah?

Would she even consider it?

A part of him wanted to believe that Julia wouldn't keep Sarah away from him forever. He wasn't a good husband, that much he knew—but he had always loved his daughter. He might've been short-tempered, even impatient at times, but he had never laid a hand on Sarah. He had tried to be a good father, even when he failed at being a decent man.

But did Julia see it that way? The realization that he had no control over this made his chest tighten. He had always been the one in control—of the house, of Julia, of how things were run. Now, all of that had been ripped away, and he was left with nothing but regret and a set of divorce papers spelling out his failures.

He stood abruptly, pacing the small living room. He couldn't just sit here and wait for Anne to be his messenger. He had to do something.

But what?

Showing up at Anne's house again wouldn't do any good. She had already made it clear that she wasn't going to give him Julia's location. And barging in, demanding answers, would only make things worse.

He needed to prove he had changed.

The thought was almost laughable—had he changed? He wasn't sure. Not really. But if he had any chance of seeing Sarah, of being part of her life, he had to start trying.

For the first time in a long while, Ed thought about things outside of his own anger and frustration. He thought about Sarah—how she must be adjusting to a new home, a new life without him. Did she miss him? Did she ask about him?

Or was she just relieved to be away from him?

The thought stung more than he expected.

With a heavy sigh, he grabbed the divorce papers and a pen. Maybe, just maybe, if he went along with what Julia wanted—without fighting, without making things harder—she'd see that he was serious. That he wanted to change.

That he wasn't ready to lose his little girl.

Ed ran a hand over his face, exhaling slowly. Letting things roll—that was his best option right now. Barging in, demanding answers, trying to force Julia's hand? That wouldn't work. It never really had.

He looked down at the divorce papers in front of him, flipping through them again. Everything was clear—custody arrangements, property division, even a line about visitation. But none of it meant a damn thing if Julia refused to let him see Sarah.

He clenched his jaw, trying to push down the frustration that bubbled up.

This wasn't about winning. It wasn't about control. It was about Sarah.

He had to prove it.

For the first time in years, he let himself acknowledge that maybe—just maybe—his temper had cost him more than he ever realized. He wasn't proud of the way he had treated Julia. He had convinced himself for so long that she just needed to listen, to do things his way. But looking back, he could see the fear in her eyes, the way she had slowly stopped talking back, stopped smiling, stopped being her.

And now she was gone.

Ed ran his hand through his hair, staring at the wall.

For now, he would let things be. He wouldn't go looking for Julia, wouldn't press Anne for more information, wouldn't try to force himself back into her life. If he pushed too hard, she'd shut him out completely.

But if he stayed calm, if he respected the distance… maybe she'd see that he wasn't the same man she left.

Maybe she'd let him see Sarah.

He had no idea how long that would take, but for once, he was willing to wait.

**

Chapter 13

Julia sat at the kitchen table, a cup of coffee in her hands, staring out the small window above the sink. The morning sun filtered through the thin curtains, casting soft light over the cozy space she had built for herself and Sarah.

Life was… settling.

For the first time in years, she wasn't walking on eggshells. The fear that had been ever-present in her chest had started to fade. She could breathe. She could think.

Sarah was adjusting well. She still asked about her daddy sometimes, but Julia had kept her answers simple. "Daddy loves you, but we needed a new home." That seemed to be enough for now.

Work was steady. The routine of her days gave her a sense of control she hadn't realized she needed. Bills were getting paid. Sarah was happy. And for the first time in a long time, Julia was happy too.

And then, there was Charles.

She smiled a little, stirring her coffee. His visit had been wonderful—comfortable, easy. He was kind to Sarah, patient with her questions, and warm in a way Julia wasn't used to. She had called him a few times since, and each time, their conversations stretched longer.

He never pushed. Never demanded anything from her. He just listened, made her laugh, reminded her that she was more than the past she had left behind.

The thought of him made her stomach flutter in a way that both excited and terrified her.

Then, her phone buzzed on the table. Anne.

Julia hesitated before picking up.

"Hey, Mom."

"Julia," Anne's voice was soft, hesitant. "How are you?"

"I'm good." And for once, she meant it.

There was a pause before Anne sighed. "I've been thinking a lot about you and Sarah. I just… I wish I had known more before you left. I keep replaying everything, wondering how I didn't see what was happening."

Julia swallowed the lump in her throat. "I didn't let you see, Mom. I was scared, and I didn't want anyone to talk me into staying."

Anne sniffled. "I should have been there for you. I should have asked more questions."

"You're here now," Julia said gently. "That's what matters."

Another pause. Then, Anne's voice wavered. "Ed came by again."

Julia stiffened. "What did he want?"

"To see you. To see Sarah."

She closed her eyes, inhaling deeply. "Did you tell him where I am?"

"Of course not," Anne said quickly. "But Julia… he seemed different. Regretful. He said he knows it was his fault. That he wants to change."

Julia's chest tightened. She had heard those words before. After every outburst, every broken promise, every cruel remark.

She opened her eyes, staring at Sarah's coloring book on the table.

"I can't let him back in, Mom."

"I know." Anne's voice was quiet. "But… what about Sarah?"

Julia exhaled slowly. That was the question she had been avoiding.

"I don't know yet," she admitted.

Anne was quiet on the other end of the line, giving Julia the space to gather her thoughts. Finally, she spoke, her voice measured but filled with concern.

"I understand, Julia. I really do. And after what you've told me, I don't blame you for wanting to keep him away. But he is Sarah's father."

Julia closed her eyes, rubbing her temple. "I know that, Mom. I do. But being her father doesn't automatically make him safe."

Anne sighed. "He said he just wants a chance to see her, to prove he can be better. Maybe he really has changed."

Julia let out a short, humorless laugh. "Or maybe he's just saying that because he lost control over us. I've heard those promises before, Mom. Every time, it was the same cycle. He'd be sorry, he'd swear he'd do better, and then it would all fall apart again."

Anne was silent for a moment, and Julia could picture her mother, sitting at her kitchen table, probably twisting a napkin between her fingers the way she always did when she was troubled.

"I don't want to push you, honey," Anne said finally. "But I also don't want Sarah to grow up with unanswered questions. Maybe—someday, not now, but someday—you can think about letting them have some contact."

Julia's stomach clenched at the thought. "I don't know if I can ever trust him again, Mom."

"I get that," Anne said softly. "And no one is saying you should right now. But if he really does want to change… maybe he should at least prove it before you shut the door completely."

Julia took a deep breath, glancing at Sarah's toys scattered on the floor. What was best for her?

"I won't let him anywhere near her until I'm sure it's safe," she said finally. "I don't owe him anything, but Sarah deserves parents who put her first. If he really wants to prove himself, he can do it from a distance."

Anne hesitated before responding. "That's fair."

There was a long pause before Anne spoke again, her voice thick with emotion. "I just want you to know, Julia… I'm proud of you. I should have seen it sooner, I should have helped more, but you got yourself out. And you're building something good for you and Sarah. I don't want you to ever doubt that."

Tears pricked Julia's eyes. How long had she waited to hear those words?

"Thanks, Mom," she whispered.

Another pause. Then Anne took a steadying breath. "So, tell me… how is Sarah really doing? And how are you?"

Julia wiped her eyes and smiled. "She's doing great. She loves her new school, and she's already made a couple of friends. And me? I think… for the first time in a long time, I'm actually happy."

Anne let out a soft laugh, one of relief. "That's all I needed to hear."

The conversation slowly shifted to lighter topics, and by the time Julia hung up, she felt… lighter.

She had made the right choice.

Now, the question remained—what was next?

**

Chapter 14

Charles had been thinking about Julia more and more. Their phone conversations had grown longer, and he found himself looking forward to every call. He had been patient, giving her space as she settled into her new life, but he couldn't ignore the pull he felt toward her.

One evening, as they talked, he finally asked, "So… how would you feel about another visit? I'd love to see you and Sarah again."

Julia hesitated for just a moment before responding. "I'd like that."

Charles smiled at the warmth in her voice. "Good. How about this weekend?"

"That works," she said, and he could hear a small smile in her voice. "Sarah will be excited. She still talks about her coloring book from the last time you were here."

He chuckled. "I'll have to bring her something new, then."

"You don't have to do that," Julia said softly.

"I know," he replied. "But I want to."

There was a pause, a comfortable silence between them, before Julia spoke again. "I'll let Mrs. Murphy know you're coming. She's been a great friend. She watched Sarah last time, and I think she'd be happy to help again if we decide to go out."

Charles noted the way she said *we*—the idea of them spending time together wasn't just his own wish anymore. She was opening up to him, little by little.

"I'd love that," he said sincerely. "I'll book a hotel again and make some plans. Any requests?"

Julia thought for a moment. "Honestly? Just something simple. Maybe dinner and a nice walk again. I liked that last time."

"Then that's exactly what we'll do."

As they wrapped up the call, Charles felt something stir inside him—**hope**. This wasn't just a friendship anymore, and he didn't think Julia saw it that way either.

This visit… it might just be the start of something more.

The evening was cool, the sky painted in deep shades of twilight as Charles pulled up to Julia's home. She greeted him at the door with a warm smile, looking more at ease than she had the last time they saw each other. Sarah, peeking from behind her mother's leg, grinned when she saw him.

"You came back!" she chirped.

"I sure did," Charles said, crouching slightly to her level. "And I brought you something." He handed her a small bag, and Sarah eagerly pulled out a new set of crayons and a sketchpad.

"Thank you!" she beamed, clutching them to her chest.

Julia shook her head with a soft chuckle. "You're spoiling her."

"She's an artist in the making," he said with a wink.

Mrs. Murphy, who had been standing nearby, stepped forward. "You two go on and enjoy your evening. Sarah and I have a whole night of cartoons and coloring planned."

Julia gave Sarah a kiss on the forehead before letting Charles lead her to his car. As they drove off, she glanced over at him. "So, where are we going?"

"Dinner first. Then… a little surprise."

She raised a brow, intrigued but not pressing for more details.

Dinner was at a cozy restaurant just outside of town, tucked away from the busy streets. Candlelight flickered on their table, and conversation flowed easily. Julia found herself laughing more than she had in a long time, losing herself in the comfort of Charles's presence.

After they finished their meal, Charles led her back to the car, but instead of heading home, he drove to a small, tucked-away place she had never noticed before.

"A bar?" she asked, glancing at the glowing sign above the entrance.

"Not just any bar," he said with a grin. "Trust me."

Inside, the place was quiet, with soft lighting and a few people scattered at tables, sipping drinks. But what caught Julia's attention was the small, intimate dance floor enclosed by white lattice panels. A single dim light hung above, casting a warm glow. The sound of the jukebox played softly in the background, just enough to hear inside the enclosed space.

Her breath caught as she took it in. "Charles…"

He held out his hand. "Dance with me?"

She hesitated for just a moment, but then she placed her hand in his. He led her to the dance floor, and as they stepped inside, it felt like they were in their own little world.

As the soft melody drifted through the jukebox speakers, Charles pulled Julia close, his hand warm and steady against the small of her back. The enclosed space, illuminated only by the dim glow above, made everything else fade away. For the first time in a long time, Julia wasn't thinking about the past or worrying about the future. She was here, in this moment, with Charles.

She let herself sink into his embrace, resting her cheek lightly against his shoulder. The steady rhythm of his breaths echoed in her ear, a sound so steady, so calm—it was nothing like the erratic, unpredictable energy she had lived with for so long.

Charles's touch was careful, never too firm, never too assuming. He held her like she was something precious, something that deserved gentleness. Julia hadn't felt that in years.

Her breath hitched unexpectedly, and she squeezed her eyes shut, willing away the sudden wave of emotion that swelled in her chest. How did something as simple as a slow dance become so overwhelming?

Charles must have sensed the shift in her, because he loosened his hold just enough to tilt his head and whisper, "You okay?"

She nodded against him but didn't lift her face. If she did, he'd see the rawness in her eyes.

"This is nice," she finally murmured, her voice softer than she intended.

"It is," he agreed, his voice low and warm. "It's been a long time since I've danced like this."

Julia let out a small, breathy laugh. "I don't even remember the last time I danced at all."

Charles pulled back slightly, just enough to look down at her. His eyes searched hers, not prying, not pushing—just looking, seeing her in a way she wasn't sure anyone had in a long time.

"You deserve this," he said simply. "To feel good. To feel safe."

A lump formed in her throat, and she swallowed hard, nodding as her fingers unconsciously tightened slightly against his shoulder. No one had ever said that to her before.

The music continued, and they swayed, lost in the quiet rhythm of the moment.

For the first time in years, Julia felt the walls she had built around herself begin to loosen, just a little. She wasn't sure where this was going, but for now, here in this tiny, glowing space, she let herself feel something she had long since forgotten.

Hope.

When the song ended, neither of them moved right away. They just stood there, holding onto the moment, holding onto each other. Then, with the softest of smiles, Charles brushed a stray piece of hair from her face.

"Ready to go?" he asked gently.

Julia took a breath, nodded, and as they stepped off the dance floor, she realized something—

She wasn't just moving through life anymore.

She was starting to live again.

As Charles pulled up in front of Mrs. Murphy's home, the porch light cast a warm glow over the small front stoop. Julia turned to him with a soft smile, the emotions of the evening still lingering in her chest.

"I had a really nice time tonight," she said, her voice quiet but sincere.

Charles returned her smile, his eyes holding something deeper. "Me too. Thank you for letting me be a part of your new life, Julia."

Her heart fluttered at his words. He wasn't pushing, wasn't demanding—just there, steady and patient.

She hesitated for a moment before reaching across the seat to give his hand a gentle squeeze. "Drive safe, okay?" she spoke softly but as Julia reached out to squeeze Charles' hand, he gently took hers and slipped a small folded paper into her palm. She looked at him, puzzled.

"What's this?" she asked softly.

Charles gave her a warm smile, his eyes full of something unspoken. "Just something to think about until I see you again," he murmured.

Charles held her gaze a moment longer, then nodded. "I will. Goodnight, Julia."

"Goodnight, Charles."

With one last glance, she slipped out of the car and walked up the steps. Before she even knocked, the door cracked open, and Mrs. Murphy smiled purposefully.

"Come on in, dear," the older woman said in a hushed voice. "Sarah's asleep on the couch. She fought it for a while but didn't stand a chance against that warm milk and bedtime story."

Julia let out a quiet chuckle as she stepped inside. "Thank you so much for watching her."

Mrs. Murphy waved a hand dismissively. "It was my pleasure. Now, tell me—how was your evening?"

Julia felt warmth rise to her cheeks as she glanced down, brushing her fingers over her wrist. "It was… nice. Really nice."

Mrs. Murphy's eyes twinkled as she handed Julia Sarah's small blanket. "That's good to hear. You deserve nice."

Julia swallowed the lump in her throat and nodded. "Thank you."

With care, she scooped Sarah into her arms, her daughter's little body curling into her instinctively. Mrs. Murphy opened the door for her, whispering, "Get some rest, dear."

As Julia carried Sarah home, the cool night air wrapped around them, and she found herself smiling. She wasn't sure where this road with Charles would lead, but for the first time in a long time, she wasn't afraid to find out.

Tonight had been more than just a date.

It had been a step forward.

Later that evening when Julia was settled in and Sarah in her bed, Julia opened the folded up paper Charles had given her in the car earlier.

My Julia,

I think of you more than I ever thought possible. You have become the rhythm of my days, the quiet melody that lingers even in my sleep. There is something about you that feels like home—like something I've always been searching for but never knew how to find. I want to be yours, always, if you'll have me, I hope one day you'll want to be mine too.

Yours,

Charles

**

The months passed, and Julia's life continued to take shape in ways she never imagined. Her relationship with Charles deepened with each visit, their bond growing stronger as trust and affection flourished. He made the long drive more often, sometimes just for a weekend, other times for a few precious hours. With every visit, he became a more significant part of her and Sarah's world.

Her job had also been a blessing. She proved herself in the assistant administrative role, earning recognition from her supervisors, which led to raises that eased her financial worries. Every extra dollar made it easier to pay the attorney fees, ensuring her divorce moved forward without delays.

And then, the court date arrived.

**

Julia sat in the courthouse waiting area, her hands folded tightly in her lap. The air smelled of old books and polished wood, the murmurs of attorneys and clerks echoing around her. Across the room, Ed sat stiffly in a chair, his expression unreadable. He had respected her space since receiving the divorce papers, and though he hadn't made trouble, she knew today would be hard.

Her attorney leaned over. "It should be straightforward, Julia. Ed didn't contest anything, so it's mostly formalities."

She nodded, but her stomach twisted anyway.

When they were called into the courtroom, Julia felt the weight of the past pressing down on her. The judge reviewed the documents, asked a few routine questions, and after what felt like an eternity—but was really only minutes—the gavel struck.

"Divorce granted."

Just like that, it was over.

Julia let out a breath she hadn't realized she was holding. She was free.

As she walked out of the courtroom, Ed approached her, his movements slow, almost hesitant.

"Julia…" His voice was softer than she expected. "I just… I want to see Sarah."

Julia met his gaze. He looked different—worn down, maybe even remorseful—but she couldn't let that sway her.

"We can talk about it," she said carefully. "But only if it's in Sarah's best interest."

Ed nodded. "I just want to do right by her."

She didn't respond right away, just studied him for a moment before turning toward the exit.

The past was behind her now.

Julia didn't rush into a decision. The idea of Ed seeing Sarah again stirred too many emotions—fear, uncertainty, and the smallest hint of hope that maybe, just maybe, he really had changed. But hope wasn't enough to go on. She needed to be sure she was making the right choice, for Sarah's sake more than anything.

So she sought advice.

First, she spoke with Sarah in the most careful way possible. One evening, as they sat on the couch, Sarah coloring in the book Charles had given her, Julia gently brought it up.

"Sweetheart, do you ever think about Daddy?"

Sarah's crayon stopped mid-stroke, and she looked up with those wide, thoughtful eyes. "Sometimes. Is he mad at us?"

Julia's heart clenched. "No, honey. He just… misses you."

Sarah seemed to consider that for a long moment before shrugging. "I miss him too… but I don't want him to yell."

That settled something in Julia's heart. If she allowed a visit, it would have to be under strict supervision.

Next, she turned to her mother.

Anne listened carefully over the phone, her voice hesitant. "I just don't know, Julia. I feel guilty every day for not seeing what was happening when you were with him. But do you really believe he's different?"

"I don't know, Mom," Julia admitted. "But Sarah deserves the chance to know her father if he really is trying. I just don't want to put her through more pain."

Anne sighed. "Then be careful. If you do this, make sure it's on your terms."

Julia promised she would.

Then, she talked to Mrs. Murphy, who had become something of a trusted confidante. The elderly woman listened quietly as Julia explained the situation over a cup of tea.

"I think you already know what you need to do, dear," Mrs. Murphy finally said. "You're a mother first, and you're protecting your child. But you also know what it's like to lose someone you love. If Ed is truly making an effort, maybe Sarah deserves to see for herself. Just be sure you're in control of the situation."

That wisdom lingered with Julia as she finally called Charles.

"I don't want to do the wrong thing," she admitted, curled up on her bed as she held the phone. "I don't trust him completely, but I do believe he wants to see her."

"I trust you," Charles said, his voice steady and sure. "You're a great mom, Julia. And whatever you decide, I know you'll do it with Sarah's best interest at heart."

That reassurance gave her the final push she needed.

The next morning, she called Ed.

"I'm willing to let you see Sarah," she said firmly. "But it will be a short visit, in a public place, and I'll be there the whole time. No exceptions."

Ed agreed without hesitation.

Julia hung up, exhaling deeply. This was a step she never thought she'd take—but she was ready.

**

The phone call had been brief but calculated. Julia had agreed to let Ed see Sarah for a short visit, but only under her terms. She chose a McDonald's in a neutral location—far enough from her home that Ed wouldn't be able to track them but public enough to ensure safety.

She didn't offer details about where she lived now, only that she'd be bringing Sarah to meet him at a place "that worked for both of them." Ed didn't push for more. Maybe he knew better than to try.

Now, she had to prepare Sarah.

That evening, as they sat curled up on the couch, Julia took a deep breath. "Sweetheart, I want to talk to you about something important."

Sarah looked up at her, hugging her worn-out bunny. "What, Mommy?"

Julia gently ran a hand over Sarah's soft curls. "Your daddy wants to see you."

Sarah hesitated, her small fingers tightening around her bunny's ear. "But we don't live with Daddy anymore…"

"No, we don't," Julia confirmed softly. "But he asked if he could see you for a little bit, just to visit. We'll meet somewhere with a play area, and I'll be with you the whole time."

Sarah's brows furrowed. "Is he mad?"

Julia's chest tightened. "No, baby. He's not mad." It was the truth—for now.

Sarah sat in silence for a moment, her little legs swinging against the couch. "Okay… but just a little while?"

Julia smiled gently. "Just a little while."

Sarah nodded, satisfied for now, and nestled against her mother's side.

As Julia held her close, she prayed that this meeting wouldn't undo all the peace they'd finally begun to find.

**

At first, Ed showed up on time, making every effort to be present for the short visits with Sarah. He brought small gifts—coloring books, stuffed animals, little trinkets he thought she might like. He asked about school, about her favorite things, and for a while, it seemed like he was trying.

But as the months passed, the visits became less frequent.

First, he rescheduled one. Then, he canceled another. Eventually, he stopped reaching out altogether.

Julia wasn't surprised. In fact, a part of her had expected it.

She watched Sarah carefully, monitoring her reactions each time a visit was postponed or missed. But Sarah never seemed heartbroken—just accepting. Maybe, deep down, she understood that some people weren't meant to stay.

One evening, as Julia tucked Sarah into bed, her daughter looked up at her with sleepy eyes and asked, "Mommy, do you think Daddy loves me?"

Julia's heart clenched. She brushed Sarah's hair back and kissed her forehead. "Aww, sweetheart. I think he just doesn't know how to be a daddy the way you need him to be."

Sarah thought about that for a moment, then snuggled her bunny closer. "That's okay," she murmured. "I have you."

Julia swallowed past the lump in her throat. "Yes, baby. You have me."

And as she turned off the light and watched Sarah drift into sleep, she knew with certainty that, no matter what, she would never let her daughter feel forgotten.

**

Chapter 15

As time passed, Julia and Charles' relationship deepened, shifting from casual visits to something steady and undeniable. He was no longer just a comforting presence—he was part of her life now. Their time together felt natural, effortless, and filled with moments that made her heart feel lighter.

Charles had always noticed her love for art, often watching as she doodled absentmindedly or sketched in the margins of her notebooks. One evening, as she sat at the kitchen table, working on a rough sketch, he leaned in and said, "You know, you really should do something with this."

She glanced at him, smiling but hesitant. "I don't know."

" Julia.,You have a gift." His voice was gentle but certain. "There's a watercolor class at the community center. You should take it."

At first, she brushed off the idea. Between work, Sarah, and simply trying to rebuild her life, it seemed impossible to carve out time for something so personal. But Charles didn't let it go.

"You've spent so much time doing what you had to do," he reminded her. "Maybe it's time you did something just for you."

That thought stayed with her, and eventually, she signed up.

From the moment she dipped her brush into the water and let the colors flow onto the paper, she knew she had made the right choice. Watercolor painting became more than just a hobby—it was an outlet, a way to express emotions she hadn't always been able to put into words. With each stroke, she poured out her past, her healing, her hopes for the future.

Charles was always there, supporting her, encouraging her, making her believe she was capable of more than she ever gave herself credit for.

One evening, after class, she sat on the porch, watching the sun dip below the horizon as Sarah played nearby. Charles sat beside her, his presence as steady as always.

"You seem different lately," he said, studying her with quiet admiration. "Lighter. Happier."

She turned to him, the warmth of his gaze sinking into her. "I think I finally am."

**

Over a year had gone by since Julia had left Ed, and in that time, she had built a life that felt safe, stable, and even joyful. Sarah was thriving, her job was going well, and her passion for watercolor painting had blossomed into something she never expected. But the biggest change was on the horizon—Charles was considering a major shift in his own life.

During one of his visits, they sat on the porch, watching Sarah chase fireflies in the dusk. Charles seemed quieter than usual, his fingers idly tracing the rim of his coffee mug. Julia noticed his pensive mood and nudged his arm gently.

"You've got that look," she teased. "Something on your mind?"

He let out a small chuckle. "I've been thinking… a lot, actually."

She tilted her head, waiting for him to continue.

"There's an opening at the local college here," he finally said. "They need a new art instructor, and I sent in an application."

Julia's heart skipped a beat. "You what?"

He turned to face her, a hopeful expression in his eyes. "I love my job, Julia. But more than that, I love being with you. I don't want to be a visitor in your life. I want to be here, really here."

Her breath caught in her throat. For so long, she had been rebuilding, creating a life she never imagined possible. And now, Charles was choosing to be part of that life in a real, tangible way.

A mix of emotions swirled inside her—excitement, nervousness, disbelief. "Are you sure?" she finally asked, her voice quiet.

"I've never been more sure of anything," he said, reaching for her hand. "If I get the job, I'll find a place nearby. No pressure, no expectations… just the chance to be close, to see where this leads without always having to leave."

Julia squeezed his hand, a warmth spreading through her chest. She had been afraid to hope for something like this, but here it was—right in front of her.

A few weeks later, Charles received the job offer. The college was thrilled to bring him on as their new art instructor, and he wasted no time making arrangements to move. Julia helped him search for a place, and before long, he had settled into a cozy home just minutes from hers.

For the first time in what felt like forever, Julia didn't feel like she was looking over her shoulder or waiting for something to go wrong. She was living, fully and completely, and for the first time, she allowed herself to believe that the happiness she had hoped for was finally coming to light.

Even though Charles now lived nearby, he didn't let the familiarity of their proximity take away from the romance. He still planned special dates, still surprised her with small, thoughtful gestures, loving notes, and still looked at her as though she was the most precious thing in the world.

One evening, he called her unexpectedly.

"Clear your schedule for Friday night," he said, a hint of excitement in his voice.

Julia smiled at the sound of it. "Oh? And what do you have planned, Mr. Romance?"

"You'll see," he teased. "Just wear something nice, and trust me."

When Friday arrived, Julia found herself feeling nervous in the best way. She slipped into a soft, flowing dress, letting herself embrace the butterflies that still came whenever she was with Charles. He picked her up right at seven, looking as handsome as ever in a crisp button-down and slacks.

"Are you ready for a night out?" he asked, offering his hand.

"Always," she said with a smile, slipping her fingers into his.

As they drove, Julia realized with a delighted flutter in her chest that they were heading back to the little tavern—the one with the intimate, hidden dance floor.

"You remembered," she whispered, glancing over at him.

"How could I forget?" he said, reaching over to squeeze her hand. "That night… I think it was the moment I realized just how deep I'd fallen for you."

Her heart swelled.

Inside, the tavern was just as warm and inviting as before. The jukebox hummed softly in the background, and the same tiny dance floor, enclosed by lattice panels and bathed in dim, romantic light, waited for them.

They ordered a drink—her a glass of wine, and him a non-alcoholic beverage since he was driving. As they sat for a moment, sipping their drinks, Julia took in the cozy atmosphere, her nerves settling under Charles' reassuring presence.

Charles turned to her, his expression tender. "Dance with me?"

Julia smiled, slipping her fingers into his.

As he led her onto the floor, the world outside faded away. The soft music wrapped around them, and he held her close, swaying gently to the rhythm.

"You still make me nervous," she admitted, resting her cheek against him.

He chuckled, his voice warm. "Good. That means this still feels as special to you as it does to me."

They moved together, slow and effortless, as if they had been dancing for years. And in that moment, surrounded by soft light and the quiet hum of a love that had grown steadily and beautifully, Julia knew she had found something real—something lasting.

When the song ended, Charles dipped his head slightly, whispering close to her ear, "I love you, Julia."

She pulled back just enough to look into his eyes, searching for any hint of hesitation. There was none.

Her heart pounded as she whispered back, "I love you too."

And just like that, the final pieces of her new life fell perfectly into place.

**

Chapter 16

Sarah

One evening, as Julia tucked Sarah into bed, the little girl clutched her ragged bunny and looked up at her mother with curious eyes.

"Mommy?" Sarah asked, her small voice soft against the quietness of the night.

Julia brushed a few strands of hair from Sarah's forehead. "Yes, sweetheart?"

Sarah hesitated for a moment before asking, "Can Charles be my new daddy?"

Julia's heart squeezed. She had known Sarah adored Charles—he had been patient, kind, and always made time for her. He never treated her like an afterthought but rather as someone who mattered just as much as Julia did.

"Do you like Charles that much?" Julia asked gently.

Sarah nodded eagerly. "Uh-huh! He colors with me, and he's funny, and he always listens to me. And he makes you happy, Mommy."

Julia swallowed against the emotion welling in her throat. "He does make me happy," she admitted with a soft smile.

Sarah grinned. "So, can he be my daddy?"

Julia leaned down and kissed her daughter's forehead. "That's a big question, sweetheart. But I promise you this—Charles loves you very much. And no matter what, you will always have people who love you and take care of you."

Sarah seemed satisfied with that for now, snuggling deeper into her blankets.

"Okay, Mommy. But I think you should ask him."

Julia laughed softly. "We'll see, baby girl. We'll see."

As she turned off the bedside lamp and closed Sarah's door behind her, she leaned against the hallway wall, her heart full, and her mind spun with the weight of her daughter's words.

She had spent so long trying to rebuild her life, never imagining it could become this whole, this filled with love.

Maybe, just maybe, it was time to think about forever.

Can Charles be my new daddy?

She had known Sarah liked Charles—adored him even—but she hadn't realized just how deeply he had woven himself into her little girl's heart. Julia had spent so much time focusing on her own feelings, her own cautious steps forward, that she hadn't fully considered how much Charles had become a presence in Sarah's life too.

Had she been blind to it? The way Sarah lit up when Charles arrived, the way she eagerly climbed into his lap to show him her latest coloring masterpiece, the way she always asked when he would visit again. She had seen it all, but she hadn't truly *seen* it until now.

Her daughter didn't just like Charles—she trusted him, she felt safe with him, and in her innocent way, she already saw him as family.

Julia exhaled, pressing a hand to her chest. Was she ready for that? For Sarah to see Charles as more than just Mommy's friend? For Charles to take on that role?

She didn't doubt his kindness, his patience, or his love. But was it fair to even consider asking this of him? Would he *want* that?

Her heart swelled with emotion—fear, hope, love—all tangled together.

One thing was clear: Charles had become more than just a part of her life. He had become a part of Sarah's too.

And now, she had to figure out what that really meant.

**

Shortly after, as Julia and Charles sat together on her small couch, she shifted nervously, turning to face him. The soft glow of the lamp cast warm light over them, but Julia felt a nervous flutter in her stomach.

"There's something I need to tell you," she began, tucking her legs under her.

Charles, sensing her seriousness, set down his tablet and turned his full attention to her. "Of course. What is it?"

She hesitated for a moment, then let out a breath. "Sarah asked me something today… something I wasn't quite prepared for."

His brows lifted slightly, curiosity flickering in his eyes. "Oh?"

"She asked if you could be her new daddy."

The words hung in the air between them. Julia searched his face for any sign of discomfort, regret, or hesitation, but instead, a gentle, almost stunned expression crossed his features.

"She *asked* that?" he said softly, as if testing the words himself.

Julia nodded. "I think I underestimated how much she cares about you. She adores you, Charles. You've been so good to her, so patient, and I guess… to her, you already feel like family."

Charles ran a hand through his hair, exhaling slowly. A small smile formed on his lips. "Wow," he murmured. "I mean, I knew she liked me, but… I didn't expect that."

Julia chewed her lip, nervous. "I don't want you to feel any pressure. She's just a little girl, and I told her that things like that take time."

He turned to her, reaching for her hand. "Julia," he said gently, his thumb brushing over her knuckles. "I love Sarah. And I love *you.*" His voice was steady, sure. "I never came into this thinking of just you and me—I always knew that Sarah was part of the package. And I wouldn't want it any other way."

Her throat tightened, emotion swelling inside her. "So… this doesn't scare you?"

He chuckled softly. "No. If anything, it makes me want to be even more present for both of you. I would never try to replace her father, but if she wants me in her life that way… I'd be honored."

Tears pricked at Julia's eyes, and she squeezed his hand. "You really mean that?"

"With all my heart," Charles assured her.

Julia let out a soft laugh, relief washing over her. "Well… I guess that means we have a lot to think about."

Charles smiled warmly. "We do. But we'll figure it out—together."

**

Later that night, as Charles lay in bed staring at the ceiling, Julia's words echoed in his mind.

"She asked if you could be her new daddy."

He turned onto his side, exhaling deeply. The thought warmed his heart in a way he hadn't fully expected. He knew he loved Julia—there had never been a doubt about that. But hearing that Sarah, sweet and innocent, saw him as something more than just her mother's friend made it all feel *real* in a different way.

He had never wanted to rush Julia, knowing she had been through so much. But now, with how settled their lives had become, how natural it felt to be with her and Sarah, he realized there wasn't anything to wait for. He *wanted* this. He wanted *them.*

Rolling onto his back again, he let out a breath and stared at the ceiling. *Maybe it's time.*

A slow smile formed as his heart settled on the decision. He would ask Julia to marry him.

**

The Proposal

It had been a quiet Saturday afternoon, and Julia had been lost in her latest painting, the soft strokes of watercolor blending seamlessly under her careful hand. Sarah was at Mrs. Murphy's for a little visit, giving Julia and Charles a rare moment alone.

Charles sat nearby, pretending to read a book, but his eyes kept drifting toward her. He had been carrying a small velvet box in his pocket for days, waiting for the perfect moment. He had replayed their journey together countless times in his head—how she had come from a place of fear and uncertainty to one of strength and confidence. How she had let him into her life, little by little, until he couldn't imagine his world without her in it.

He finally stood and walked over to her, gently setting a hand on her shoulder. "Take a break for a second?" he asked softly.

Julia looked up, paintbrush still in hand, a playful smudge of blue paint on her wrist. "From this? You know how I get when I start something."

"I do," he chuckled, then hesitated. "But I think I have something more important than painting to talk about."

Her brows furrowed slightly, but she set her brush down, giving him her full attention. Charles reached into his pocket and slowly pulled out the small box, opening it to reveal a delicate ring. The moment the light caught the diamond, Julia's breath hitched.

"Julia," he said, his voice steady but full of emotion. "From the moment I met you, I knew you were special. Watching you grow, seeing you find your happiness again—it's been the greatest privilege of my life. I love you, and I love Sarah. I want to spend forever with both of you."

Tears welled in Julia's eyes as she covered her mouth with her hand, overwhelmed.

He took her hand gently. "Will you marry me?"

A tear slipped down her cheek, but her smile was radiant. "Yes, Charles. A thousand times, yes."

With a relieved chuckle, he slid the ring onto her finger, then pulled her into his arms, holding her as if he never wanted to let go.

In that moment, Julia knew she was exactly where she was meant to be.

**

Chapter 17

Painting

Julia found herself lost in the colors that danced across her canvas. Her strokes had grown more confident, her blending more fluid. What had once been just a hobby was now something more—a true passion she allowed herself to embrace.

She had shared some of her paintings with Teresa, Sarah's sitter, as well as Mrs. Murphy and a few coworkers, each of them offering kind words and encouragement.

"You have such a gift," Teresa had told her one afternoon while Julia picked up Sarah. Teresa had been flipping through a few of her paintings that Julia had brought over. *"These are incredible, Julia. Have you ever thought about selling them?"*

"These belong in a gallery, dear," Mrs. Murphy had added another time, admiring a soft landscape Julia had painted of a sunrise over rolling hills. *"You have real talent—don't let it go to waste."*

Even her coworkers had taken an interest. One day in the breakroom, she had mentioned her love for painting, and before she knew it, they were asking to see her work. Their reactions had been overwhelming.

"I'd buy this in a heartbeat," one had said.

"You should do an art show," another suggested.

Julia had laughed at the idea, but the more she thought about it, the more it didn't seem so impossible. Painting had been a form of healing for her—a way to express emotions she hadn't been able to put into words. Maybe, just maybe, it was time to take it a step further.

That evening, she found herself sitting at her small kitchen table, flipping through the pages of paintings she had carefully stored. A new thought began to take root.

Maybe it was time to truly share her art with the world.

Julia smiled to herself as she flipped through her paintings, running her fingers lightly over the edges. She had been hearing so much encouragement lately—Teresa, Mrs. Murphy, even her coworkers—but Charles had been telling her for a long time how talented she was. *"Julia, your work is incredible,"* he had said more than once, studying her pieces with an admiration that made her cheeks flush. *"You put so much feeling into your art—it's more than just skill, it's emotion on canvas. You need to share this."*

At first, she had brushed off his words, thinking he was just being kind. But he had never stopped believing in her, even when she doubted herself. When she hesitated to show others, he was the one who encouraged her, reminding her that her work deserved to be seen.

Now, with so many voices echoing the same sentiment, she couldn't ignore it any longer.

Maybe Charles had been right all along.

Maybe it was time to stop just painting for herself.

Maybe it was time to share her art with the world.

One evening, as Julia and Charles sat together in her cozy living room, she took a deep breath and finally voiced what had been on her mind.

"Charles," she started, tracing the rim of her coffee mug with her finger, "I've been thinking… maybe it's time I actually show my paintings. You've always told me I should, and now, with everyone else encouraging me too, I feel like maybe… maybe I should take that step."

Charles set his cup down and turned to her, his expression warm with encouragement. "Julia, that's amazing," he said. "I've been waiting for you to believe in yourself the way I believe in you. Do you have any ideas on where you'd like to start?"

She exhaled a small laugh. "That's the thing—I have no idea. I mean, you have connections in the art world, way more than I do. I wouldn't even know where to begin."

Charles nodded thoughtfully. "I do know a few gallery owners who love discovering new talent. There's an upcoming local art showcase in a couple of months—nothing too overwhelming, but enough to get your work seen. I could talk to the curator, see if they have space for a few of your pieces."

Julia's eyes widened. "Really? You think they'd be interested?"

"I don't think, Julia—I know," he said, his voice full of certainty. "Your work speaks for itself. Let me make a few calls, and we'll go from there."

Julia felt a rush of excitement and nerves all at once. This was it. The first real step toward something bigger. And with Charles by her side, she knew she wouldn't be taking it alone.

**

A few days later, Julia found herself in the art studio, cleaning off her brushes after finishing a new piece. Her instructor, Margaret, a spirited woman with a no-nonsense attitude, walked up behind her and took a long, approving look at the watercolor.

"You know, Julia," Margaret said, crossing her arms, "I don't think I've ever had a student pick up watercolor techniques as naturally as you have."

Julia chuckled, wiping her hands on a rag. "Well, I've had a good teacher."

Margaret waved off the compliment. "I can teach all I want, but you're the one bringing the paintings to life. Every time I push you to try something new, you take it and run with it. And then what happens?" She raised an eyebrow expectantly.

Julia smiled, already knowing the answer. "Someone wants to buy it."

"Exactly!" Margaret clapped her hands together. "It's almost like you're afraid to admit you're a real artist. But guess what? You are, Julia. You're selling your work. People are drawn to it. That's what artists do!"

Julia sighed, glancing at the painting in front of her. It was a misty landscape with soft hues of blue and lavender. The kind of piece she never would have attempted months ago, but Margaret had encouraged her to push past her comfort zone.

"You really think I'm ready to put myself out there?" she asked, her voice quieter now.

Margaret softened. "I don't just think it—I know it. Charles knows it, your friends know it, and deep down, I think you know it too."

Julia let that sink in. Between Charles' connections and Margaret's constant push to grow, it was getting harder and harder to deny that maybe, just maybe, she was meant to do this.

**

Chapter 18

The Wedding

The day of Julia and Charles' wedding was a reflection of who they were—simple, intimate, and full of love. Julia didn't want anything extravagant, just a day surrounded by the people who had become her family. The ceremony was held in a small chapel on the edge of town, its white wooden walls and stained-glass windows glowing warmly in the afternoon light.

Sarah was beaming as she stood beside Julia in a pale yellow dress, clutching a tiny bouquet of daisies. She had been overjoyed when Julia told her that Charles was going to be her daddy, and she had spent the past few weeks talking about how she couldn't wait for them to be a real family.

Mrs. Murphy sat in the front row, dabbing at her eyes with a lace handkerchief, and Teresa, Julia's trusted babysitter, smiled proudly as she watched. Even Anne had come, her heart finally at peace knowing her daughter had found the love and security she deserved.

Julia's dress was simple yet elegant—a flowing ivory gown with delicate lace along the sleeves. She had no veil, just her hair softly curled and pinned to the side. When she stepped into the chapel and met Charles' gaze, the warmth in his eyes made every struggle, every fear, and every painful moment of her past feel like a distant memory.

The ceremony was short but heartfelt. When Charles took Julia's hands and vowed to love and cherish her, she felt the weight of all she had been through lift away.

"I promise to always stand beside you, to encourage your dreams, and to build a life filled with love and laughter," Charles said, his voice steady with emotion.

Julia blinked back tears. "And I promise to love you with my whole heart, to trust in the future we're creating, and to always hold onto the faith you gave me—that tiny mustard seed of faith you handed me when we first met, the one that reminded me to believe in something better."

When the officiant pronounced them husband and wife, Charles gently cupped her face and kissed her, sealing not just their vows but the journey that had brought them together.

The reception was held in a cozy garden behind the chapel, where strings of soft lights hung from the trees and simple mason jars filled with wildflowers decorated the tables. There was no grand banquet, just a home-cooked meal shared among friends and family. The music was soft, the laughter genuine, and as the evening wore on, Julia found herself dancing in Charles' arms under the warm glow of the garden lights.

Sarah twirled around them, giggling as she danced with Mrs. Murphy, and for the first time in as long as Julia could remember, she felt nothing but peace. She had a new life, a new love, and most importantly, a future she was excited to wake up to every single day.

**

Settling Into Married Life

The weeks following their wedding were filled with small, beautiful moments as Julia and Charles settled into married life. They decided to stay in Julia's small mobile home for now—it made sense. Sarah was comfortable there, her sitter, Teresa, was nearby, and Mrs. Murphy had become a second grandmother to them. It wasn't about the size of the home, but rather the warmth within it.

Charles brought over his belongings bit by bit, careful not to overwhelm the space. His books now lined a small bookshelf in the corner of the living room, and his easel found a spot beside Julia's near the window where the morning light streamed in. Their shared love of art made their home feel like a creative haven, where inspiration always had a place to land.

Sarah adjusted well to having Charles there more permanently. She adored him, clinging to his side during evening story time and excitedly helping him cook breakfast on the weekends. "Now we're like a real family," she had said one night at dinner, her little voice full of innocent happiness. It made Julia's heart swell with gratitude.

Of course, there were small adjustments—Julia had been on her own for a while, and Charles had never lived with a child before. There were moments of figuring out routines, balancing work, parenting, and their own time together. But it all fell into place naturally, as if this was always how it was meant to be.

One evening, after Sarah had gone to bed, Julia and Charles sat curled up on the couch, the soft glow of a single lamp illuminating the room. Julia leaned her head on his shoulder, sighing contentedly. "Did you ever think your life would look like this?" she asked softly.

Charles smiled, pressing a kiss to the top of her head. "Not exactly, but I can't imagine it any other way now."

Julia reached into her pocket and pulled out a tiny locket, one she had bought shortly after Charles first gave her the mustard seed of faith. She had recently, carefully, placed the seed inside it, keeping it close to her every day as a reminder of the strength and faith that had carried her here. She turned it over in her fingers before looking up at Charles.

"I never told you," she said quietly, "but I carry it with me still. The mustard seed you gave me."

His eyes softened as he looked down at the delicate locket in her hands. He gently traced his fingers over it before taking her hands in his own.

"It was never just about the seed," he murmured. "It was about believing that even the smallest bit of faith could grow into something beautiful."

She swallowed past the lump in her throat and nodded. "And it has."

He kissed her then, slow and sweet, sealing in the moment that was filled with love, gratitude, and the quiet promise of forever.

**

Chapter 19

The Art Show at The Butterfly

The day of the art show had arrived, and Julia could hardly believe it. Her work—her paintings—were being displayed in *The Butterfly*, a charming little local gallery that had quickly become a favorite among artists and collectors in the area. It was a place known for showcasing new talent, and thanks to Charles' encouragement and her art teacher's persistence, Julia had been given a spot in their latest exhibit.

As she and Charles entered the gallery, the warm lighting reflected off the soft cream-colored walls, where various paintings hung in perfect arrangement. Julia's section was set up beautifully, featuring a range of her watercolor pieces—landscapes, delicate floral arrangements, and even a few portraits that had become some of her best work.

Sarah, dressed in a sweet little blue dress, held Julia's hand tightly, her eyes wide with excitement. "Mommy, look! Your paintings are here!" she whispered in awe.

Julia laughed softly, squeezing her daughter's hand. "They sure are, sweetheart."

Mrs. Murphy had insisted on coming, her face beaming with pride as she admired the paintings. "I knew you had something special, dear," she said, patting Julia's arm. "These paintings have life in them. People will see that."

As the evening progressed, guests strolled through the gallery, stopping to admire the pieces, some discussing them in quiet appreciation. Julia was nervous at first, but as people approached her, asking about her inspirations and techniques, she began to relax. She loved talking about her art—it was her passion, after all.

Then, something unexpected happened.

A woman in a stylish blazer with an air of confidence approached Julia. "Your work is stunning," she said, offering her hand. "I'm Eleanor Hayes, an art collector and gallery owner. Have you ever considered selling your pieces beyond local exhibits?"

Julia's breath caught for a moment. "I—well, I've sold a few pieces here and there, but I've never really thought about anything bigger."

Eleanor smiled. "You should. Your style is unique, and I know a few galleries that might be interested in featuring your work."

Julia felt Charles' hand gently rest on the small of her back, his quiet support giving her the strength to say, "I'd love to hear more about that."

The conversation continued, and by the end of the night, Julia had not only sold three of her paintings but had also exchanged contact information with Eleanor, opening a door she never imagined walking through.

As the event wound down, Julia stood back and looked around, taking in the moment. This wasn't just an art show—this was a turning point.

Charles leaned in and whispered, "See? I told you your talent would take you places."

She smiled up at him, feeling the mustard seed pendant in her pocket. Faith had brought her here. Love had given her courage. And now, a new chapter was about to begin.

**

A Meeting with Eleanor Hayes

A few days after the art show, Julia sat at her small kitchen table, staring at Eleanor Hayes' business card. The woman's words had lingered in her mind, stirring something inside her—excitement, curiosity, and a touch of fear.

Charles, sitting across from her with a cup of coffee, noticed her hesitation. "You're overthinking it, aren't you?" he asked with a knowing smile.

Julia exhaled a laugh. "Maybe a little. I mean, what if I'm not ready for something like this?"

Charles reached for her hand, squeezing it gently. "You are. You've worked so hard, and this could be an amazing opportunity. Besides, you don't have to commit to anything right away. Just hear her out."

Nodding, Julia picked up her phone and dialed the number on the card. It rang twice before Eleanor's polished voice answered, "This is Eleanor Hayes."

"Hi, Ms. Hayes, this is Julia Schiff. We met at *The Butterfly* gallery the other night."

"Julia!" Eleanor's voice warmed instantly. "I was hoping I'd hear from you. How are you?"

"I'm doing well," Julia said, glancing at Charles, who gave her an encouraging nod. "I wanted to follow up on our conversation about expanding my work beyond local exhibits. If you're still interested, I'd love to set up a meeting."

"I was just about to suggest the same," Eleanor replied. "Would you be available to meet this Saturday afternoon? I'll be in town and would love to discuss some opportunities with you."

Julia felt her heart pick up speed. "That sounds perfect. Where should we meet?"

"There's a lovely little café downtown called *Latte Junction*. It's quiet, and they make an excellent latte," Eleanor said. "Would two o'clock work for you?"

"That works perfectly," Julia agreed.

"Wonderful. I look forward to it, Julia."

As Julia ended the call, she let out a deep breath and looked at Charles. "Well, it's happening. I have a meeting."

Charles grinned. "And you're going to be amazing."

Julia smiled, but inside, nerves still fluttered. Was she truly ready for this next step?

**

The Meeting at The Latte Junction

The small café had a warm, inviting atmosphere—exposed brick walls, soft lighting, and the comforting aroma of fresh coffee and pastries. Julia arrived a few minutes early, smoothing her blouse as she stepped inside. Her eyes scanned the room until she spotted Eleanor Hayes at a corner table, dressed elegantly in a navy blazer, a notebook and a latte in front of her.

Eleanor looked up and smiled as Julia approached. "Julia, wonderful to see you. Please, have a seat."

"Thank you," Julia said, settling into the chair across from her. A waiter soon arrived, and she ordered a vanilla latte, her hands resting in her lap as she gathered her thoughts.

Eleanor leaned in slightly, her expression warm yet professional. "I'm so glad you reached out. I meant every word at the gallery—your work has a rare emotional depth that speaks to people. Have you ever considered selling your art beyond small exhibits?"

Julia hesitated. "I mean, I've thought about it, but I never imagined how to make that happen. The idea of going beyond local shows feels… a little overwhelming."

Eleanor nodded with understanding. "That's completely natural. But you have the talent, Julia. I work with a network of gallery owners, collectors, and buyers who are always looking for fresh, authentic art. Your watercolor work, especially those pieces inspired by nature and personal experience, could do very well in broader markets."

Julia sipped her latte, processing Eleanor's words. "What would that look like, exactly? I mean, how would I even start?"

Eleanor pulled out a sleek planner and flipped to a page with handwritten notes. "First, I'd like to feature a few of your pieces in an upcoming exhibit I'm curating in a larger city gallery. That would give your work exposure to a broader audience. If that goes well, we can discuss placing some of your art in a permanent collection or even launching an online presence for sales."

Julia's heart pounded. Her work… in a real gallery, beyond her small town? It was a thrilling but intimidating thought.

Eleanor smiled at her hesitation. "I'm not asking for an answer right this second. Take a few days to think about it. Talk to Charles, your family, whoever you need to. But I truly believe this could be the start of something incredible for you."

Julia nodded slowly, excitement flickering beneath her nerves. "Thank you, Eleanor. I appreciate the opportunity—and your belief in my work."

"Of course," Eleanor said, standing and extending her hand. "Let's stay in touch. I'll send you the details about the exhibit, and you let me know what you decide."

As Julia walked out of *The Latte Junction*, the cool afternoon breeze hit her face, grounding her. She pulled her tiny pocket locket from her purse, feeling the mustard seed inside. Faith. The same kind Charles had given her when she was just beginning to believe in herself again.

Maybe, just maybe, this was the next step she was meant to take

**

Julia's Internal Struggle

As Julia drove home, Eleanor's words replayed in her mind. A broader audience. A real gallery. An online presence. It all sounded so… big. Bigger than she had ever imagined for herself.

Her hands gripped the steering wheel a little tighter as doubt crept in. What if my work isn't good enough? What if the people in those larger galleries don't see the value in it like Eleanor does?

She had spent so long building a quiet, stable life for herself and Sarah. The idea of stepping into something unknown, something with expectations and potential failures, sent a wave of uncertainty through her. She had finally found peace—was it worth risking that for a dream she wasn't even sure she deserved?

And then there was Charles. He had always been her biggest supporter, encouraging her to push past her self-doubt. What will he think? Will he tell me to go for it? Will he be disappointed if I let fear hold me back?

Her mind spun between excitement and hesitation, but as she pulled into the driveway of their little home, she reached into her purse and traced her fingers over the tiny locket that held her mustard seed.

Faith.

She had taken a leap before—leaving Ed, starting over, building a new life. She had faced fear head-on and came out stronger.

Maybe it was time to take another leap.

**

Julia Talks to Charles

Later that evening, as Sarah lay asleep in her bed, Julia Sat on the couch next to Charles, tucking her legs beneath her. The room was softly lit, casting warm shadows on the walls.

Charles noticed the quiet way she was fidgeting with the hem of her sweater and set down his book. "Alright," he said with a teasing grin. "I know that look. Something's on your mind."

She let out a small laugh, shaking her head. "Am I that obvious?"

"Only to someone who knows you," he said, nudging her knee with his own. "Tell me."

Taking a deep breath, she recounted her meeting with Eleanor—her offer, the gallery show, the potential of expanding her art beyond their small town. As she spoke, she avoided his gaze, afraid of what she might see there.

When she finally finished, she braced herself for his reaction.

But when she finally looked up, she found nothing but pride in his eyes.

"Julia," he said, his voice full of warmth, "this is amazing. This is exactly what you deserve."

She exhaled, a mixture of relief and lingering fear. "But what if I'm not ready? What if it's too much? What if I fail?"

Charles reached out and took her hands in his. "You're already doing it. People already love your work. And if you fail? Then you learn from it, grow, and try again. But I don't think you're going to fail, because you have something rare—your art isn't just skill, Julia. It's heart." "It's the beauty of your soul flowing out onto the watercolor paper, the beauty that you have shared with me and now have the opportunity to share with many others."

She bit her lip, feeling the weight of his words. "You really think I can do this?"

He smiled, lifting her hands and pressing a kiss to her knuckles. "I don't just think it—I *know* you can."

A warmth spread through her chest, the doubts still lingering but not as heavy. Maybe she *could* do this. Maybe, with Charles by her side, she could take that leap after all.

**

The Winslow Gallery Show with Eleanor

The night of the gallery show arrived faster than Julia expected. The past few weeks had been a whirlwind of preparation—choosing the right pieces, framing them, pricing them, and coordinating with Eleanor. She had spent countless nights in her small art space, perfecting every last detail, her nerves mounting with each passing day.

Now, standing outside *The Winslow Gallery*, she took a slow, measured breath. The elegant script of the sign above the entrance glowed softly in the evening light. Through the wide windows, she could see people milling about, wine glasses in hand, admiring the artwork. *Her* artwork.

Charles squeezed her hand. "You ready?"

She let out a small, nervous laugh. "I don't think I'll ever be fully ready."

"Good thing you don't have to be. You just have to step inside," he said with an encouraging smile.

Taking one more deep breath, she nodded. "Okay. Let's do this."

**

Inside the Gallery

As they walked in, Eleanor greeted Julia with a warm smile and a gentle squeeze of her arm. "You made it right on time."

Julia took in the sight before her. The walls of the gallery displayed her paintings beautifully—soft landscapes, delicate florals, and serene water scenes. She could hardly believe they were hers. Small placards beneath each one bore her name. *Julia Schiff.* Seeing it written there, displayed so professionally, made it all feel real.

Guests were already moving through the space, stopping to admire her work, murmuring to one another. A few even held brochures with her name and artist statement printed on them.

"This is incredible," she whispered, her fingers tightening slightly around Charles's.

"That's because *you* are incredible," he murmured back.

Before she could respond, a woman approached her. "Are you the artist?" she asked, eyes warm and excited.

Julia hesitated for a split second before nodding. "Yes, I am."

"Your work is *stunning*," the woman said. "I was just telling my husband that your use of color has such a calming effect. There's so much emotion in each piece."

Julia's cheeks warmed. "Thank you so much. That really means a lot."

As the woman moved on, Eleanor leaned in. "See? You *belong* here."

A mixture of nerves and joy swirled in Julia's chest. Maybe she did belong.

**

The night of Julia Schiff's gallery show at *The Winslow* was nothing short of extraordinary. From the moment the doors opened, guests filled the space, admiring her work and engaging in thoughtful conversation about her paintings. The air buzzed with excitement, and Julia could hardly believe how many people had come to see her art.

One by one, red dots were placed beneath her paintings. Each sale sent a wave of emotion through her—excitement, disbelief, gratitude. She watched in awe as strangers connected with her work, sharing their interpretations and personal stories about what the paintings made them feel.

Eleanor Hayes, approached Julia with a pleased smile. "This is just the beginning for you," she said confidently. "Your work speaks to people, and I'd love to feature you again in the future."

Julia could only nod, still trying to process everything. Charles, standing nearby, caught her eye and grinned. "Told you," he whispered.

As the evening wound down, Julia took a quiet moment to soak it all in. She had dreamed of this, but never truly believed it would happen. Now, with her artwork finding homes and new opportunities ahead, she felt something she hadn't in a long time—certainty.

Slipping her hand into her pocket, she felt the tiny locket that held the mustard seed of faith Charles had given her. She smiled softly. It had started as a symbol of hope, but now, it was proof of how far she had come.

**

Chapter 20

Life Moves On

A few years had passed since Julia Schiff's first gallery show at *The Butterfly*, and her career had flourished beyond what she ever imagined. Her paintings were now displayed in multiple galleries, and collectors sought her work. With each passing year, her confidence as an artist grew, and she found joy in every brushstroke.

Her life with Charles was just as fulfilling. Their love had only deepened over time, as their lives intertwined more deeply, Julia and Charles found themselves dreaming of a home that truly reflected their growing life together. The small home they shared had been a place of healing and new beginnings, but with Julia's art flourishing and Charles full time teaching position, they both felt the pull for something bigger. Not extravagant—just a place that would give them the space to breathe, create, and continue building their future.

They began searching for a home in the same area, ensuring that Sarah's routine remained unchanged. She would still have Teresa as her sitter, and Julia could remain close to Mrs. Murphy, whose presence had been a quiet pillar of comfort throughout the years. Eventually, they found the perfect house—a cozy yet spacious home with an extra room that would become their shared art studio, filled with natural light from large windows. Sarah would finally have a bigger bedroom, one she could decorate however she pleased, making it truly her own.

As they packed up their old home, Julia couldn't help but reflect on how far she had come. This move wasn't about escape or survival; it was about embracing a future built on love, creativity, and stability—things she had once thought impossible. And as they turned the key to their new home for the first time, hand in hand, she knew in her heart they had made the right choice.

As the months passed, Julia, Charles, and Sarah settled comfortably into their new home. The extra space brought a sense of ease to their lives—Sarah loved having a bigger bedroom to decorate as she pleased, and the art studio quickly became a cherished retreat for both Julia and Charles. The large windows bathed the room in natural light, making it the perfect space for creativity to flourish.

Julia's art continued to thrive, with each gallery show bringing new opportunities and more recognition for her work. Collectors and art lovers alike were drawn to her paintings, and with Charles's encouragement, she found herself more confident in sharing her talent with the world. Meanwhile, Charles's job at the college had transitioned from an adjunct position to full-time, securing their future even further. Teaching had always been a passion of his, and now he had the chance to fully invest in guiding young artists while still dedicating time to his own work.

Life was good—better than Julia had ever imagined it could be. Their home was filled with warmth, love, and laughter, and for the first time in years, she felt truly at peace.

But then, something changed.

**

Chapter 21

It started subtly. Charles would brush off his exhaustion as overwork, his headaches as stress. But Julia noticed—how he winced when he moved too quickly, how his appetite dwindled, how his vibrant energy had dulled. At first, he assured her it was nothing, just getting older, just life.

But as weeks turned to months, the symptoms became harder to ignore. The once strong and steady Charles, who had always been the one to encourage and uplift her, now seemed weighed down by something he wouldn't name.

One evening, as Julia prepared dinner, she caught him leaning against the kitchen counter, his breathing heavier than usual. Concerned, she turned off the stove and reached for him.

"Charles, something isn't right," she said softly. "Please, let's go see a doctor."

He gave her a small, tired smile. "Jules, I don't want you to worry."

"But I am," she admitted, her voice trembling. "I can't just stand by and watch you struggle. Please."

Charles held her gaze for a long moment before nodding. "Alright," he finally said. "We'll make an appointment."

Julia exhaled in relief, but deep down, fear had already settled in her heart. Something told her this wasn't just exhaustion. Something was truly wrong.

Charles's fatigue and discomfort persisted, and Julia's concern deepened with each passing day. He still insisted it was nothing serious—just the wear and tear of life—but Julia knew better.

Then came the moment she couldn't ignore. One evening, after a long day at the college, Charles walked into the house, looking paler than usual. His usual warm smile was strained, and as he sat down at the table, she noticed the way his hands trembled slightly. When she placed dinner in front of him, he barely touched it.

"Charles," she said gently, sitting beside him, "this isn't just stress. You're not yourself."

He sighed, rubbing his forehead. "Jules, I don't want to make a big deal out of this."

"But it *is* a big deal," she insisted. "You're exhausted all the time, you're losing weight, and you've barely been eating. Please, let's get you checked out."

He hesitated, but then he saw the worry in her eyes—the same eyes that had always seen the best in him, that had trusted him when she had every reason not to trust anyone. Finally, he nodded. "Okay," he said quietly. "I'll go."

Weeks later, they sat in a doctor's office, waiting for answers. Charles had gone through a series of tests, and now they were about to hear the results. Julia's hands were clasped tightly together in her lap, her stomach twisting with unease.

Dr. Noble, a middle-aged man with kind eyes, folded his hands on the desk and looked at them with measured calm. "Charles, based on your test results, it appears that your kidneys are not functioning as they should. Your creatinine levels are high, and there are signs of significant kidney disease."

Julia felt her breath catch, and she instinctively reached for Charles's hand. "What does that mean?" she asked, her voice barely above a whisper.

Dr. Noble gave them both a sympathetic look. "It means we need to take action. Your kidney function is low enough that we need to consider dialysis soon. We'll also discuss long-term options, including the possibility of a transplant."

Charles was quiet for a long moment, his expression unreadable. Then he let out a slow breath and gave a small nod. "Alright," he said, his voice steady. "What do we do next?"

Julia squeezed his hand, holding back the wave of emotions threatening to overwhelm her. She had feared bad news, but hearing it confirmed it still sent a sharp ache through her chest.

Dr. Noble outlined the treatment plan—dietary changes, medication, and the need to start dialysis within the next few months. The reality of it all settled heavily between them.

That night, when they returned home, Julia made sure Sarah was asleep before stepping onto the back porch with Charles. They stood in the quiet of the evening, the stars scattered across the sky above them.

"Are you scared?" she finally asked, her voice soft.

Charles exhaled slowly. "A little," he admitted. "But mostly, I just don't want this to change everything. I don't want you worrying over me all the time."

She turned to him, her eyes filled with determination. “You don’t get to decide that, Charles,” she said. “I *will* worry. I *will* be here. We’re in this together.”

He looked at her for a long moment before pulling her into his arms, pressing a gentle kiss to her forehead. “I love you, Julia.”

Tears welled in her eyes as she held onto him. “I love you too. And we’re going to get through this.”

She didn’t know what the road ahead would look like, but she knew one thing for certain—she wasn’t going to let him face it alone.

**

Charles adjusted to life with kidney disease as best he could. At first, he managed well—following dietary restrictions, taking medications, and keeping up with his work at the college. But as time went on, his energy waned. Fatigue became a constant companion, and soon, the doctors confirmed what he and Julia had been dreading: he would need dialysis.

The first dialysis session was the hardest. Julia sat beside him in the clinic, holding his hand while the machine did the work his kidneys no longer could. His expression was calm, but she saw the exhaustion in his eyes.

"Well," he joked weakly, "this isn’t exactly how I pictured a romantic outing."

Julia forced a smile, squeezing his hand. "Yeah, well, you still owe me a proper one after this."

He chuckled, but they both knew the reality they faced.

Life changed. Dialysis treatments took over their routine, leaving Charles drained three days a week. Julia adjusted her work schedule to be there for him, but even with their best efforts, the weight of his illness settled over their home.

Sarah, now a teenager, noticed everything. She was no longer the little girl who accepted simple reassurances—she wanted answers.

"Mom," she asked one evening, crossing her arms as she leaned against the kitchen counter, "is Charles going to die?"

Julia inhaled sharply. "Sarah..."

"Don't sugarcoat it," Sarah interrupted. "I see how tired he is. I hear you crying at night when you think I'm asleep."

Tears pricked at Julia's eyes. She set down the dish she had been drying and turned to her daughter. "I don't know what's going to happen. But what I do know is that we love him, and we're going to be here for him every step of the way."

Sarah blinked rapidly, her tough exterior cracking. "I don't want to lose him."

Julia pulled her into a hug. "Neither do I, sweetheart. Neither do I."

**

Some days, Charles had enough energy to take Sarah out for coffee or sit with Julia while she painted, offering quiet observations about her work. Other days, he barely made it out of bed, his body too drained from treatment.

One evening, after a particularly rough day, he sat on the couch staring at a blank canvas Julia had set up for him.

"I used to love painting," he murmured. "I keep thinking I'll pick up the brush again, but I just… I don't have it in me."

Julia sat beside him, resting her head on his shoulder. "Then let me paint for both of us."

He smiled faintly. "I'd like that."

Sarah walked into the room, settling in between them she took a paintbrush in hand "You know, you could at least tell me what to paint. I mean, I am the daughter of an artist."

Charles chuckled. "Alright, missy. Paint me a sunset."

Sarah smirked. "Only if you promise to hang it up.", knowing she had no clue how to paint.

**

A Ray of Hope

The doctors mentioned a kidney transplant as a possibility, but the waiting list was long. Julia, desperate to do anything, got tested to see if she was a match.

When she got the call, her heart pounded.

"Mrs. Schiff," the nurse said, "I'm sorry, but you're not a match for Charles."

Julia swallowed the lump in her throat. "Is there anything else we can do?"

"We'll keep looking. In the meantime, it's important that he continues dialysis and follows his treatment plan. We'll notify you the moment we find a donor."

She thanked the nurse and hung up, her hands trembling. Charles was running out of time, and she was powerless to change it.

That night, as she lay beside him, she whispered, "We'll find a way. I promise."

Charles squeezed her hand. "I already have everything I need, Julia. I have you and Sarah. That's more than enough."

In the doorway, Sarah lingered, watching them. She hadn't meant to overhear, but hearing Charles' words solidified something in her heart.

The man who had once been just her mother's friend had become her father in every way that mattered. And now, as much as she wanted to believe love would be enough, she knew—deep down—that time was slipping through their fingers.

**

As the months passed, Charles' condition worsened. By the time winter arrived, dialysis was no longer enough. His body was growing weaker, and the doctors had warned them that without a transplant, his time was limited. Julia and Sarah did everything they could to keep life as normal as possible, but reality hung over them like a dark cloud.

By early spring, Charles had stopped teaching. The college gave him a quiet farewell, honoring him with kind words and appreciation, but Julia saw the sadness in his eyes. Teaching had been his passion, and letting it go felt like losing another piece of himself.

Despite his declining health, he still made an effort to keep their life together as steady as possible. He and Sarah would watch movies together on the nights he had energy. Julia would sit by his side, painting as he rested, and he'd offer quiet comments between his naps.

One evening, as the sun dipped below the horizon, he reached for Julia's hand.

"Promise me something," he murmured.

She looked at him, brushing her thumb over his knuckles. "Anything."

"When I'm gone… don't stop painting."

Tears welled in her eyes, she nodded, but never spoke a word.

**

The Last Weeks

By summer, Charles was bedridden. His body, once strong and full of life, had become frail. Hospice care had been set up in their small home, and Julia refused to leave his side. Sarah, now nineteen, had grown into a compassionate young woman, balancing her own life with being there for the man who had become like a father to her.

She helped wherever she could—adjusting pillows, reading to him, and sitting quietly when he was too tired to speak. At night, when the house was quiet, Julia would listen to his breathing, holding onto every moment, knowing their time was slipping away.

One evening, as the warm breeze drifted in through the open window, Julia sat beside Charles, her fingers tracing the edge of that small trinket she had carried for years, the tiny locket that held the mustard seed he had given her long ago.

She opened it, looking down at the tiny symbol of faith, then reached for his hand.

"You gave me this when I needed it most," she said softly, her voice thick with emotion. "But what I didn't realize back then was that *you* were my faith, Charles. You believed in me when I didn't believe in myself. You saw a future for me when I couldn't see past my fear."

His tired eyes met hers, and though he was weak, he managed a small smile. "You didn't need me to believe in you, Julia. You just needed someone to remind you of what was already there."

She leaned down, pressing a kiss to his forehead. "I love you," she whispered.

His fingers curled around hers. "I love you too."

A few days later, on a quiet morning in late July, Charles took his final breath.

He was at home, in the bed he shared with Julia, with Sarah curled up in the chair beside him. Julia held his hand, whispering how much she loved him until the very end.

One last breath, and then, he was gone.

**

Chapter 22

The funeral was small and intimate, attended by friends from the college, neighbors, Mrs. Murphy, and even Eleanor Hayes from the gallery. Anne held Julia as she wept, while Sarah stood quietly beside her, strong yet grieving.

Throughout the service, Julia kept her hand wrapped around the tiny locket that held the mustard seed—Charles's first gift to her, the symbol of the faith he had given her in herself. She had carried it through every challenge, every triumph, and now, even in her loss, she held onto it tightly.

As the ceremony ended, a gentle breeze stirred around them, warm and familiar, as if Charles was still near.

Walking back to the car, Sarah slipped her hand into Julia's.

"What do we do now, Mom?" she asked softly.

Julia exhaled, glancing at the locket resting in her palm before closing her fingers around it.

"We keep going," she said, her voice steady despite the ache in her heart.

Sarah nodded, gripping her mother's hand tighter.

And so, through grief and love, they took their first steps forward—together.

**

Chapter 23

Lost in the Silence

The days blurred into one another, each one an echo of the last. Julia woke up, but only because her body forced her to. She brewed coffee out of habit, yet it grew cold on the counter, untouched. She moved through the house like a shadow of herself, drifting from one room to another without purpose. The home, once filled with warmth and love, felt unbearably empty.

She still went to work every day, but only because she had to. Her job provided routine, a place to go, a distraction—but that's all it was. The motions were automatic: answering calls, filing paperwork, attending meetings. Smiling when expected, speaking when necessary. No one at work spoke of her loss unless she brought it up first, and she never did.

She still went to the gallery, but not because she wanted to—only because it was expected. Framing, packaging, responding to inquiries—it was all mechanical, just tasks to complete. She no longer painted though. Her brushes sat stiff in their cups, the watercolors dried on their palettes, her easel coated in a fine layer of dust. The vibrancy of her art had faded, just like everything else in her life.

Sarah called every day, her voice lined with worry, but Julia reassured her with hollow words that she was fine. Mrs. Murphy knocked on her door often, bringing meals she barely touched. Even Eleanor gently urged her to return to painting, to let her emotions pour onto the canvas, but

Julia couldn't. The colors didn't speak to her anymore. Her world had turned to only shades of gray.

Everything inside the house remained just as Charles had left it. His coffee mug still sat on the counter, his favorite book with his reading glasses resting on top of it, waiting for hands that would never pick it up again. His scent still lingered on the sweater draped over the back of the chair, a cruel reminder of what she had lost.

And the nights—oh, the nights were unbearable. The bed was too big, too cold. The silence pressed in, suffocating her, stretching endlessly as she lay awake, clutching the mustard seed locket against her chest.

She whispered his name into the darkness, "Charles, Charles my love, I miss you," hoping—praying—that somehow, somewhere, he could still hear her.

But the emptiness never answered back.

**

A few weeks had passed, though time felt meaningless to Julia. The days blurred together, each one an echo of the last. She went through the motions—work, home, sleep—yet everything felt hollow, like she was merely existing rather than living.

One evening, as she moved through the house, her steps slowed near the doorway of the art studio. She hadn't entered since Charles passed. But each time she walked by, her eyes were drawn to it, lingering for just a moment longer than the time before.

Tonight, she stopped.

The dim hallway light cast a glow into the room, illuminating the two easels standing side by side. Hers, untouched, gathering dust. His, still holding the last canvas he had worked on—a landscape left unfinished, waiting for brushstrokes that would never come.

Her chest tightened as she stepped inside. The air smelled of oil paint and aged wood, scents once comforting but now steeped in sorrow.

Her fingers brushed against Charles' easel, tracing the dried paint along the edges. Everything was exactly as he had left it. The brushes still sat in their jars, the palette bore the last colors he had mixed, and his stool remained slightly pulled out, as if he had only just stepped away.

She swallowed hard, her gaze shifting to her own easel. The blank canvas stared back at her, a silent invitation. But she felt nothing. No spark. No desire. Just an emptiness that painting could never fill again.

With trembling hands, she turned away and opened the storage cabinet. One by one, she gathered her brushes, her paints, her palettes, and placed them inside. She hesitated only once—her fingers hovering over the worn wooden box that held her watercolors, the ones Charles had given her.

But even those, she closed inside.

Finally, she reached for a sheet and draped it over both easels, hiding them from view.

She had believed painting was a part of her, that it was something she could never walk away from. But standing there now, she knew the truth.

That part of her was gone…Just like Charles

**

Closing the Door on the Past

Time moved on, though Julia barely noticed. Days stretched into weeks, then months, yet the ache in her chest remained as heavy as the day she lost Charles. She carried it with her, an invisible weight that dulled everything around her.

Still, the pull of the art room never truly left her. Every time she walked past it, she felt it—a quiet whisper calling her back, a ghost of the life she had once shared with Charles. But she refused to listen.

Those paints she had tucked away in the storage cabinet still lingered, waiting. She knew they were there, as if they had a presence of their own, murmuring her name in the stillness of the house.

She didn't want to hear them anymore.

One evening, after another long day at work, she stood in the doorway of the art room, staring into its quiet stillness. Dust had begun to gather on the covered easels, the air held the faint scent of old paint, and yet it no longer felt like a space that belonged to her. It was a reminder of everything she had lost, a part of a world she no longer belonged to.

Taking a deep breath, she stepped inside.

She moved with careful precision, as if handling fragile memories. One by one, she gathered the things that had once been her passion—the brushes, the paints, the palettes. The canvases, both blank and unfinished. Even Charles' easel, the last piece of him she had left untouched.

She packed them all into a large box, sealing them away like a chapter of her life she could never return to.

Then, with quiet determination, she carried the box up the narrow attic stairs.

The attic was dimly lit, the air thick with the scent of time and forgotten things. Julia found a space in the corner, tucked beneath the beams, and set the box down. She traced her fingers along the lid one last time before stepping away.

As she descended the stairs, she closed the attic door behind her.

Painting was no longer a part of her world.

She even disconnected from the galleries, cutting ties with that life completely. She let go of the shows, the buyers, the people who had once admired her work. It didn't matter anymore. That Julia—the one who had painted with passion, the one who had believed in art—was gone.

And she had no desire to find her again.

**

The Mourning

Though Julia was only in her early forties, the thought of loving someone else never crossed her mind. Love, for her, had been defined by Charles—his kindness, his patience, the way he had seen her even when she couldn't see herself. What they had was rare, irreplaceable. No one else could ever measure up.

She spent many evenings lost in thought, sitting by the window as the sun dipped below the horizon, remembering him. The way he had smiled at her from across a room, the sound of his laughter, the warmth of his embrace. Those memories were enough. They had to be.

She still kept the mustard seed, a symbol of the faith he had once given her when she had none. But now, rather than keeping it tucked away, she placed the tiny locket onto a delicate chain and wore it daily. The chain draped long so that the locket rested just over her heart, a quiet, constant reminder that he was still with her in the only way he could be.

Time moved forward, but Julia stayed still in the ways that mattered most. She had loved once—deeply, fully, and with everything she had. That was enough.

Nights were the hardest. The quiet wrapped around her like a heavy, suffocating blanket, pressing down on her chest, making it hard to breathe. She sat curled up in Charles' old chair, the fabric worn in places where his hands had rested, where his body had shaped it over the years. She ran her fingers over the armrest absentmindedly, as if somehow, she could still feel his warmth there. But it was cold—everything was cold without him.

The house, once filled with laughter and soft conversation, felt hollow now. The ticking clock on the wall marked the time, indifferent to her sorrow. She had lost track of how many evenings she had spent like this, staring at nothing, lost in memories. She could still hear his voice in her mind, picture the way he used to look at her, the way he would reach for her hand without thinking, just because he wanted to touch her.

She clutched the locket around her neck, the small mustard seed inside resting against her skin. It had once been a symbol of hope, of faith in herself, in their love. Now, it felt like a relic of a life she no longer belonged to. What was she supposed to believe in now? The man who had given her courage was gone.

Tears welled up in her eyes, but she didn't wipe them away. She just let them fall, soaking into the fabric of the sweater she wore—the one that had belonged to him, the one that still faintly smelled of him no matter how many times she washed it.

She whispered his name into the silence, knowing there would be no answer. And for the first time since he had passed, she allowed herself to admit the truth she had been too afraid to say out loud.

"I don't know how to do this without you."

Still, she spent her remaining years drifting through life—one day, one week, one month, one year at a time. The world moved forward, but she remained in place, caught somewhere between the past and the present. She adjusted to being alone, learning how to fill the silence with books, old movies, and quiet walks through town. But no matter how much time passed, just the mention of Charles' name would bring tears to her eyes.

Sarah stayed close, checking in on her often, always making sure she wasn't too alone. Julia appreciated her daughter's love and concern, but even Sarah couldn't fill the emptiness that Charles had left behind. Julia smiled when she needed to, reassured Sarah when she worried, and carried on as best as she could. But deep down, she knew—some loves are once in a lifetime, and Charles had been hers.

**

Chapter 24

Julia Goes Home

Sarah had always dreaded this moment, but no amount of quiet preparation could have braced her for the reality of it.

She had let herself into the house like she always did, calling out, *"Mom?"* as she set her purse down on the entryway table. There was no answer, but that wasn't unusual. Sometimes, Julia was reading or napping, lost in her own world. But today, the air felt different—too still, too silent. A strange chill ran down Sarah's spine as she stepped further inside.

Then she saw her.

Julia sat in Charles' old chair, her hands folded neatly in her lap, her head resting slightly to the side, as if she had simply fallen asleep. The soft glow of afternoon light streamed through the curtains, casting a golden hue around her. Her mother looked peaceful, more at ease than Sarah had seen her in years. And yet, Sarah knew before she even touched her—before she even knelt beside the chair and whispered, *"Mom?"*—that she was gone.

Julia had aged to her mid 80's and had spent 44 of those years without Charles. She mourned each and every day, but was finally rejoined with him. The calmness of her expression, the ease, it's almost like she was happy finally, with Charles at last.

A sharp gasp broke from her lips as reality crashed in. *No, no, no, not yet…* Tears burned her eyes as she reached for Julia's hand, her fingers trembling. It was cool to the touch, but still,

Sarah clung to it, her heart pounding as if she could will her mother back, as if sheer love could undo the inevitable.

A sob broke free from her chest, then another. *She was just here. I just talked to her. She can't be gone.* But the truth sat heavy in the silence. Julia had left this world just as she had lived in it since losing Charles—quietly, with little fanfare, slipping away into the memories she had cherished more than life itself.

Sarah's gaze dropped, and that's when she saw it.

The mustard seed locket.

It lay against her mother's heart, just as it always had. Sarah reached out, brushing her fingers over the tiny locket, her vision blurred with tears. That small, simple token that Charles had once given Julia all those years ago—it had never left her. Even in death, she had held onto the love that had given her strength, given her faith.

Sarah let out a shaky breath, a painful mix of grief and understanding settling into her chest. *She missed him too much. She never really stopped waiting for the day they'd be together again.*

And now, she was.

With one last sob, Sarah leaned forward, resting her forehead gently against her mother's shoulder. *I love you, Mom. I hope you're finally home—finally with Charles.*

**

The small chapel was filled with a mix of people from every chapter of Julia's life. The art world, which she had once distanced herself from, now came to pay their respects, artists and gallery owners who still admired her work even after she had stepped away. Neighbors from the mobile home park, the ones who had watched her rebuild her life and find happiness with Charles, sat quietly, some dabbing their eyes.

Her family was there—Rick, standing with a solemn expression, Sarah clutching a tissue in her hands, her eyes red-rimmed from days of mourning. And then there was Ed. He stayed toward the back, a shadow among the crowd, making no attempt to approach but unable to stay away. His face was lined with regret, his posture tense, as though he knew he didn't belong yet felt compelled to be there.

Sarah saw him but said nothing. This wasn't about the past. Today was about honoring her mother, the woman who had endured, who had loved deeply, and who had finally found peace after so many years of mourning Charles, she was now with him in eternity.

**

Chapter 25

The Bittersweet Goodbye

A few months had passed since Julia's funeral, and now Sarah found herself in the bittersweet task of preparing her mother's home for sale. Room by room, she sorted through Julia's belongings, each item holding memories that tugged at her heart. The house felt unbearably empty without her mother's quiet presence, and every creak of the floor reminded her of what was now lost.

As she climbed up into the attic, a wave of dust swirled in the dim light. The space was filled with old boxes, forgotten keepsakes, and the weight of the past. She had nearly finished sorting through everything when she spotted a box tucked in the corner. Something about it made her pause.

Pulling it toward her, she brushed away the dust before carefully lifting the lid. Inside, as she expected, were her mother's old paints, brushes, and a few well-worn canvases. But beneath them, nestled together like a hidden treasure, was a small stack of folded notes. Her pulse quickened as she picked one up, recognizing the handwriting immediately. It was Charles'.

Her hands trembled as she unfolded one of the notes and began to read:

*"My Dearest Julia,

Every day with you is a gift I never take for granted. You are the color in my world, the warmth in my coldest nights, and the whisper of hope when I need it most. You once told me I was your faith, but the truth is, you are mine. Loving you has been the greatest joy of my life, and I would choose you in every lifetime, in every universe, in every breath I take.

Forever yours,

Charles"

A sob broke from Sarah's lips as she pressed the letter to her chest. Even after all these years, their love felt alive within these words. She looked down at the paints—her mother's passion, buried in grief. A thought flickered through her mind.

Maybe some things weren't meant to be packed away forever.

Sarah carried on with emptying the house, moving from room to room, each space echoing with the ghosts of laughter, love, and moments that had shaped her life. Every chair, every framed picture, every worn-in spot on the floor held a memory so vivid she could almost reach out and touch it. Some made her smile, others made her chest ache, and some left her standing still, eyes closed, just breathing it all in.

The kitchen, where she and her mom had shared so many heart-to-hearts over cups of tea, felt unbearably silent. The living room, where Julia had sat quietly in Charles' chair, lost in her own world of longing, felt like a space frozen in time. Sarah ran her fingers along the edge of the old wooden table, remembering the nights they had sat here playing cards, talking about life, and leaning on each other through the hardest days.

The weight of it all pressed against her, as heavy as the wet, salty warmth rolling down her cheeks. The memories were beautiful, filled with love, but knowing there would never be another one made it nearly impossible to keep it together.

As she stood in the doorway of her mother's bedroom, she let out a shaky breath. This was the hardest part. The bed was still neatly made, the way Julia always kept it, the faint scent of her perfume lingering in the air. Her mother had spent so many nights alone here, missing Charles, holding onto the past while time carried her forward.

Sarah swiped at her tears and took another deep breath. She had a job to do. Her mother's house—the place that had been filled with so much love, loss, and healing—would soon belong to someone else. But no matter where life took her, she knew one thing for certain: the love that had filled these walls would stay with her, always.

Sarah stood there, her arms wrapped around herself as if trying to hold in all the emotions threatening to break free. The house was nearly empty now, but it still felt full—full of memories, of love, of the life her mother and Charles had built together.

Her gaze drifted toward the chair where Julia had taken her last breath, where she had finally found peace, finally reunited with the love she had spent years aching for. A fresh wave of tears welled in Sarah's eyes, blurring the view of the home she had once run through as a child, the home where laughter and love had echoed through the walls.

She swallowed hard, her throat tight with grief, and whispered into the stillness, her voice soft and broken from crying, "I love you, Mom… and Charles."

The words hung in the air, met with nothing but silence, yet she felt them—felt them as if they were standing beside her, arms around her, whispering back,

We love you too.

Epilogue

The sun hung low in the sky, casting a warm golden glow over Hopetown. A soft breeze rustled the trees outside as Sarah stood on the porch of her mother's now-empty home. It had taken months to sort through everything, to decide what to keep and what to let go of. But some things were never meant to be left behind.

In her hands, she held the box from the attic—the one filled with Julia's paints, brushes, and the letters Charles had written over the years. She had read each one, tracing the words he had so carefully written, feeling the love they shared echo in every stroke of ink. Love like theirs didn't fade with time; it endured, whispered in the wind, carried in the hearts of those left behind.

Sarah glanced down at the mustard seed locket now hanging from her own neck. Her mother had worn it every day, carrying that tiny seed of faith next to her heart. Now, it rested against Sarah's chest, a reminder of everything her mother had been—strong, kind, full of love, even when life had tried to break her.

She looked out at the horizon, her heart both heavy and light. Julia and Charles were together now, and though she missed them, she knew their love hadn't truly left. It lingered in the brushstrokes of her mother's paintings, in the notes Charles had written, in the memories woven into every corner of this small town.

Taking a deep breath, Sarah turned and stepped off the porch. There was still life to be lived, stories to be told. And though she walked forward alone, she carried with her the love of two souls who had shaped her own.

A love that would never fade.

Thank you for reading my story of Julia's journey to HOPETOWN.

We each have our own journey through this world and I wish you happiness on yours.

US National Domestic Violence Hotline

Call 800-799-7233

Made in the USA
Columbia, SC
08 April 2025

56253927R00115